NIGHT
MAZE

Also by Annie Dalton

Out of the Ordinary

Annie Dalton

NIGHT MAZE

Teens · Mandarin

First published in Great Britain 1989
by Methuen Children's Books Ltd
Published 1990 by Teens · Mandarin
an imprint of Mandarin Paperbacks
Michelin House, 81 Fulham Road, London SW3 6RB

Mandarin is an imprint of the Octopus Publishing Group

Text copyright © 1989 Annie Dalton

ISBN 0 7497 0322 9

A CIP catalogue record for this title
is available from the British Library

Printed in Great Britain
by Cox and Wyman Ltd, Reading, Berkshire

For my children:
Anna, Reuben and Maria.

'Nature alwaies intendeth and striveth to the perfection of Gold, but many accidents comming between change the mettals.'

From The Mirror of Alchimy, attributed to Roger Bacon 1597

Contents

1

Norah's Ark

'No,' said Gerard furiously. 'No – I'm staying here. I'm staying here.'

So this was what he'd been dreading for the last three days. This was what Lark had been leading up to with her maddening signs and portents.

'Norah's back,' Phil had yelled through the door. 'She wants to see you when you're decent.'

And that was when Gerard knew for sure.

The bad times were starting up all over again. The good times were over. It had just been a question of time.

Norah looked all in. She had a headache, he thought, and was trying not to show it. Half a cigarette was already burning in her ashtray. She had kicked off her posh tight shoes and cupped her hands around her steaming POISON coffee mug, warming them. Usually Norah dressed as if out of some kind of nostalgia for school uniform: navy round-necked jumpers, grey flannel skirts, checked Viyella shirts and flat shoes. But today she was wearing a proper dress and tights and small pearl studs in her ears. If he had seen her setting off in the morning he'd have known there was something up right away.

'Why didn't anyone tell me?' he demanded.

'I knew he'd feel like this,' said Phil wretchedly. 'You

should have warned him, you know.' He stood at the uncurtained window, fingers pressed against the glass. The darkness came right up to the house with a bluish, almost electric quality to it, though the moon was hidden.

Gerard was cold and clammy from having to dive into his clothes straight from the bath. He'd had to jam his dirty socks into his pockets in the rush. Norah's sisal carpet prickled under his damp bare feet. His skin felt wrong as if it had lost its fit. Everything felt wrong.

'Why didn't they want me before? What's changed all of a sudden? It was before that I needed them. When I was little. When my mum died. Not now. Not now I've got a decent place to live.'

'They're your family, Gerry. Your mother's family.' Norah ran both hands through the shaggy pepper and salt thatch of her hair as if she wanted to tear the front bits out. All the kids at Deben House knew it was Norah who held the whole crazy place together, year after year. Amongst themselves they didn't call it Deben House. They called it Norah's Ark. Seeing gruff unsinkable Norah even temporarily at a loss terrified Gerard.

She was talking to him but part of him was still in the bathroom listening to Phil hammering on the door, his heart pounding, his skin turned to goose-flesh.

He'd fled to the bathroom in the first place to get away from them all and get some peace, but peace wasn't to be had. After all these years Lark was back inside his head, pestering him to listen to her. He realised she only wanted to warn him something was up, but nowadays he preferred his warnings in solider, more conventional form. Everyone else outgrew these kinds of unofficial manifestations after they'd been at

10

Deben House for a few months, but for some reason not Gerard.

It was too much like being a vulnerable small child again. So he'd tried to ignore her, drown her, by talking a bit louder than usual, watching more TV. He even started going out running, slogging along for miles in the Suffolk countryside, telling himself he was just getting into training for the cricket season.

But it had never been easy to outmanouevre Lark. When he carried on refusing to acknowledge her, she just stepped up her guerrilla activities and simply found more ingenious ways to take her gentle revenge. Just minutes before he fled upstairs to the bathroom, she doctored the pieces on the Scrabble board. Phil was looking the other way, gloomily surveying his own letter tiles, obvious rejects from a Serbo Croat edition of the game, and didn't see what happened.

LARK said the letters on the board. And then – GOLD, CURSE, they'd amplified, unhelpfully. He'd swear he hadn't put them there. In the old days when he was still glad to have her around, when he'd still needed her, she quite often sent him secret messages via the school blackboard or a grimy window pane, to reassure him that he really would survive till home time. He was the only person who ever saw them of course. Well, all right, *imagined* them. Imaginary friends. Small lonely children had them. It happened all the time.

But he was fourteen. He was fourteen today. Today had been his birthday. That was why Norah should have been there. It wasn't the lack of present he minded, though he'd good reason to hope she'd picked up his gentle hints about wicket-keeping gloves. It was the way Phil insisted they had to start the celebrations without

11

her. The way Mrs Grist kept looming lopsidedly at him from under the balloons, all teeth and orange hair dye, as if about to unleash some devastating news that would change the shape of his world forever. She'd just been at the sherry, Gerard told himself, to get herself in a party mood. It wouldn't be the first time.

But Phil was sober, stone cold sober, and still couldn't look him properly in the eye. Phil always looked everyone in the eye. With years of experience of sensing catastrophe well before it had the chance to take him by surprise, Gerard took this as a sign of chilling ill omen.

Norah put her hand, warm from the coffee mug, over his own, startling him back into the room. 'I know it's hard for you to take it in,' she was saying in her hoarse Hartlepools. 'But they've been looking for you for a long time. They want you, Gerard. And a few weeks ago a firm of solicitors in London managed to track you down. Well, no, Gerard – ' She leaned back in her chair and rubbed her eyes hard. 'That isn't quite honest of me. It's actually my fault. I saw the advertisement in the newspaper and I contacted them.' She looked unhappy. 'I should have asked you. Normally that's what I would have done. But I followed my instincts the way I usually do and my instincts are usually reliable and right.'

'Not this time,' said Gerard. 'This time, Norah, they couldn't have been wronger. If you had asked me I'd have told you. I like it here. It's nice. Please tell them that and ask them to forget all about me and leave me alone. They can't be that great anyway or my mother wouldn't have been living all on her own with me in some lousy rented room.'

Now he knew why he'd always secretly liked the way

the children called it Norah's Ark. It rattled and rocked along in all kinds of weather but inside you were always warm and dry, out of reach of the flood. He was happy here. He was happy. The thought of Deben House to come home to at the end of the school day, draughty, tatty perhaps but breathing out familiarity and welcoming security – that made up for everything. After the foster homes, finding himself living with Norah had been like coming out of a blizzard into the warm and being dried all over with a rough towel.

It was true that it was almost always chaotic. Someone was almost always throwing a tantrum or going through a Difficult Phase. But even that was now so familiar to him that there was a peculiar kind of safety in it. Emotions that would have exploded like grenades, flattening into rubble frailer, nicer households than Norah's, here blew themselves out like passing squalls and moved off, leaving the furniture intact, the roof undamaged. And Norah was still there; slightly more battered than before, perhaps, but still unshocked, unjudging. Whatever you said, whatever you did, however outrageously angry you were, however panic-stricken, Norah had seen it all before and Norah's Ark could take it.

'They aren't real family. If they're so wonderful why didn't they help her? Why was she left all alone with me? That isn't family,' he said, almost shouting at Norah. 'I don't think that's family.'

'I met your uncle,' said Norah quietly. All this while she hadn't touched the cigarette, consuming itself wastefully in the air. Now she picked it up and took a couple of quick shaky puffs as if she needed them. 'He drove down to London to meet me. I told him I'd have to talk to you and that you might not want to have anything to do with them. I said that even if you did, there would have to be a long and careful period of introduction on both sides. But I did think you might at least give them a chance.'

Your uncle. He had an uncle. Since he was two years old there had been no one and now, suddenly, an uncle real enough, solid enough to drive out of the mists in a real car and ask questions about his nephew at a real solicitor's office.

'No,' he said aloud. 'No. Sorry and everything. Do you mind if I go now? I've just had a bath and I dried myself in a hurry and I'm really cold.'

He shivered to show her just how cold. 'I just want to go to bed. Sorry, Norah, if you've had a bad day because of me. Sorry.'

He had his hand on the door knob.

'He gave me some photographs,' said Norah. 'You might like to look at them when you're by yourself. That doesn't commit you to anything, does it?'

Oh didn't it! He couldn't be caught like that. He was half out of the door now, and it wasn't just the door into the hall but the door to everything known and safe. Nearly home and dry, he thought. No harm done. If Lark would just leave him alone, stop messing about with his mind, and playing word games. GOLD, CURSE, he thought, involuntarily.

'No thank you,' he said politely. 'Sorry, Norah.'

And he closed the door.

Phil and Norah looked helplessly at each other.

The door opened.

'Yes,' said Gerard, not looking at anyone. 'All right. I may as well look at them. Let me see them.'

* * *

14

It was impossible to sleep. His mind was so stuffed with new information about himself. He felt queasy, exhausted, but at the same time wildly awake as though a 100 watt light bulb had snapped on inside his skull.

Owlcote. That was the name of his family home. A castle. Or as good as. A great fortified Elizabethan house built by his own ancestors. He'd no idea his mother had come from that kind of family. He knew that kids in homes sometimes cherished grandiose fantasies but he'd always thought of his mother as poor because of how she'd been living when she died.

He sat up, remembering the photograph, its shine worn off long ago with fingering, hidden under his socks in his chest of drawers. He turned his lamp softly to the wall, so that it wouldn't wake Errol, who shared his room.

Errol rustled uneasily under his quilt, sighing like wind down a drain, but when a few moments passed without anyone leaping up with eyes like cartwheels, howling about spooks and vampires, Gerard judged it safe to dig around cautiously in his drawer until he found her picture. Then he sat on his bed for a long while, staring at it in the lamplight.

When he had been living in the Midlands, one of the foster mothers kept asking him if he didn't want to visit his mother's grave and put some flowers on it. He didn't. The idea terrified him. The same foster mother said Gerard was withdrawn, sullen and ungrateful and she could never tell what he was thinking. Once he said anxiously to Norah when they were on a shoe-buying expedition: 'Don't you ever want to know what I'm thinking?'

And she gave a surprised bark of a laugh and said,

'Why ever should I? Your thoughts are your own affair. People aren't winkles to be prised out of themselves with pins. They open when they're ready and not before.' Then they ate new sugary doughnuts from the Bread Kitchen and Norah bit into the exact jammy epicentre of hers and splattered them both with lurid red cherry jam. He had to lend her his handkerchief to clean them both up.

The young woman's face gazed elusively past him. *Lindsey*, he said inwardly, trying vainly to summon her. Maybe he remembered her eyes. It was hard to tell. Probably she was the sort of person who suddenly feels unbearably shy when she has to face a camera. He did himself. She wasn't deliberately avoiding his eye. She hadn't meant to die. She had been hurrying home to him with cough medicine and antibiotics. She had only slipped out for ten minutes. She hadn't wanted to make him worse by taking him out on such a cold winter's day. She had loved him, he thought. But to his guilt and sorrow he couldn't remember her at all. It was as if, when she died, all his early life had been torn away from him, blown clean across the universe like a scrap of old newspaper and lost forever.

Even when he thought about the way she died, senselessly knocked down by a speeding car, the only things that came to mind were stupid things with no rhyme or reason to them; the way apples smelled when they were baking, a snatch of a dim-witted music-hall song about Daisy and a bicycle made for two.

He put the photograph back under his socks, gently bumping his fingers against something small and hard. That was the other thing he had of hers.

In the old foster home days, Lark and Gerard had

16

invented a whole series of deeply satisfying secret games about it. Lark called it the Gift. Now he caught himself childishly pretending that Lindsey had brought it with her from Owlcote for a reason. That it always meant something special to her. That Lindsey always intended Gerard to keep it. As though she had finally managed to get a message to him from her distant star, like light that takes years to travel. A message without words. Sign and symbol of her love for him. But it was only an old-fashioned bobbin made of bone. There wasn't even any thread on it. Some inheritance. His eyes smarted as he pushed it to the back of the drawer. Imaginary friends. Stupid games. He was fourteen. *Fourteen*. He switched out the light.

'Owlcote,' he whispered into the dark, summoning up again that unimaginably huge ivy-clothed house with its lofty towers and flying buttresses; its great ancient trees.

'Uncle Avery,' he said softly. But he wasn't in the photographs. Perhaps he had been behind the camera. In the photographs there were two tiny little fair haired twins in identical jogging suits and trainers, and there was their mother, Aunt Caroline. She was dark haired and wearing a flowered, softly gathery sort of dress like the mothers who sometimes waited outside Gerard's school in their Volvos. Aunt Caroline was smiling directly into the camera with none of his own mother's apparent nervousness. That is, her mouth was smiling. Her eyes seemed a bit vague, he remembered. She looked nice though. And his younger uncle was there, Uncle William, in old jeans and a Fair Isle sweater, grinning amiably like a big kid.

But he was sure Norah said *three* cousins. Lawrence

17

and Flora were the twins. Imagine lumbering some poor kid with the same name as a tub of soft margarine. They must be planning to send her to private school. Harriet. That was the other one. Good grief – Harriet! She wasn't in the photographs either. Probably out riding her bloody pony in the park.

But he had a family. An amazing fairy story family. And they wanted him. They wanted him to go and live with them and be part of them.

But they don't know me, he thought in fear. He pictured himself: short, mousy, too pale-faced in last year's mud-coloured anorak which had been marked down because of being slightly faded from the shop window.

Feeling suddenly physically sick he began, drearily, to catalogue his inadequacies. He was dull. He was nothing to look at. He was stupid at school. Stupid at all school things. All he could do was play cricket and make brilliant scrambled eggs and omelettes. That wasn't enough. It wasn't enough to impress anyone.

I'll tell Norah they've got to forget about me, he thought, in a vain attempt to trick himself into relaxing and falling asleep.

But how could he, now, forget about them?

Once when he was small and lonely, Lark had opened a door in the air and through it showed him another world. He could never afterwards remember what he had seen, only the feeling of profound relief that the life he was living was not the only life there was; it had given him strength, the knowledge that he could always choose to open a door in the air and step through it into a different life. But now a door had opened without his choosing, without his wanting it, and even if he locked it up tight again and threw away the key he couldn't forget it was there. He'd always wonder what was behind it, waiting.

Tossing and turning and sighing, Gerard at last fell asleep.

In his dream he was small again and a woman with her back to him was unfastening the doors of cage after cage to let the birds fly out into a wet spring morning. He thought the woman might be his mother but just as she was going to turn round so he would finally know for sure, Mrs Grist came slamming in and it was time to get up.

Somehow, without knowing how, unless Lark had been busy while he was asleep, Gerard found he had come to a decision.

'I'll give it a try,' he said. 'I'll go. But I don't want to be slowly and carefully introduced if you don't mind, Norah. I think I'd go mad if I had to do it like that. If they're sure they really want me – I'll go. And if it doesn't work out – '

Norah hugged him hard. 'You know there's always room for you here,' she said. 'But it will work out. I can't explain how I know but I do. Your uncle seemed so delighted to have traced you after all this time and there was a young woman there, Beatrice Summers. She's qualified recently as a lawyer apparently and is also a friend of the family. She – '

But Gerard wasn't listening. He was too dazed by his own accomplishment. He'd done it. He'd set something in motion. He'd made a wave and now off it went, rushing, gathering power, curling over and over away from him in an endless succession of new waves, utterly out of his control.

'Will you tell them?' he asked. 'Will you phone my — my uncle,' he tripped over the unfamiliar word, 'and tell them?' Then as he was leaving her room, he said on impulse, 'Is he nice, my uncle? Did you like him, Norah?'

Norah replied in her hoarse, smoked kipper voice that of course he was nice. There was nothing for Gerard to worry about at all. Uncle Avery was a perfectly nice, kind man, only slightly resembling Blue-beard and therefore probably didn't own a locked chamber full of secret horrors.

Gerard went out laughing at his own previously nameless anxieties and Norah gruffly chortled along with him. But as the door closed she found herself reflecting uneasily that it had actually been Beatrice Summers generating most of the warmth and enthusiasm. And perhaps unwittingly it was Norah herself, still, after all these years a sucker for happy endings, who supplied the rest.

Uncle Avery agreed to everything that was said and done, but apart from that, sat wrapped in his own private silence, unless asked a direct question or otherwise prompted to give an opinion.

It was lively Beatrice, with her wide smiling mouth and dangling earrings like windchimes who lingered in Norah's memory; Beatrice who gave Norah most of the personal information she needed about the Noones and their household. (Norah had also gained the entirely unofficial impression that Beatrice had a bit of a thing for Avery's younger brother, William.) It was Beatrice who expressed the family's regret and sorrow about Gerard's mother, Lindsey. It was Beatrice who could not quite manage to hide the tears that sprang to her eyes.

But Avery Noone sat unmoving and apparently unmoved – as cut off from the give and take of ordinary human exchange as a remote fog-shrouded island off the coast of Nova Scotia.

But be fair, everyone has off-days, thought Norah. The poor man probably had a headache after the long drive. And I know, I do know that Gerard needs to go back amongst his own family. He'll do better there. It'll bring him out of himself. He'll have the chance to do something with his life. I know that it's the right thing.

She lit another cigarette and puffed away at it hungrily, a stern, elderly schoolgirl. Oh how I hate all this damn playing at God we have to do in this business, she thought. Who am I kidding? I don't know anything. Anything at all.

2

Leavetakings

It was all arranged. By tomorrow nothing would ever be the same again. His uncle Avery was coming to fetch him in the morning.

When he fell asleep at last it was almost to his surprise since it felt like settling down for a doze on the outermost ledge of a mountain precipice.

He was running. Running in the dark down narow paths that twisted and doubled back on themselves. He had to get there, this time he had to get there on time. But the whole point of this dream was that he never did. Suddenly, within the nightmare, he came curiously awake recognising both the place and the fear that saturated it like old bloodstains and he knew he had been dreaming this dream all his life.

Which door? Which door? said the voice, the one that wanted him to understand everything.

You'll always be too late, said the other voice unpleasantly. The one that knew he would fail. *There's nothing you can do, Gerard Noone. It will all have to happen over and over again. You'll always be too late and it will go on happening again and again. Face facts. Some things can never be changed. What can you do? What could you possibly do?*

But on he ran, compelled to try yet again, running and sobbing with the shame of his inadequacy and the dread of what waited for him at the end of the dream. He could hear the voice now, the blank, hardly human voice singing the words which explained everything if only he could understand.

'Earth, Water, Fire, Air. Met together in a garden fair. Put in a basket bound with skin – '

He was almost there. If he could just make it round the next corner.

There she was! He could save her. She had only just unstoppered the bottle. She was putting back her head ready to swallow. This time he could prevent her. Her unwashed hair hung around the small empty face in rat's tails. Her old-fashioned shift was torn and filthy.

'No – ' he cried. 'No – You mustn't. Please don't!'

But it wasn't any good. He was still too late. She had sunk so deeply into herself she couldn't even hear him. If only he could have got close enough to *touch* her –

'Oh no – Don't!' he screamed.

For now it was beginning, now and again and forever and nothing could change it. From the soles of her bare dirty feet to her bony chest, to the ragged ends of her fingernails, she was changing, changing: the dull stain seeping upward, soaking upward, invading, usurping the colour of living human flesh, the unwashed linen, invading, emptying.

From another path a man broke from the darkness, a burning torch in his hand, his face smeared with soot and smoke, his leather apron charred and torn.

'You're too late,' cried Gerard in anguish. 'Look!'

But before it reached her throat the girl half-turned to the man, gasping out, 'Now will you love me?'

And then Gerard turned and fled so that he could not see her lifeless golden arms forever reaching out, the expression of terror forever printed on her golden face. And the tearing sobs of the great burly man following him as he ran blindly this way and that, lost forever in the maze.

He woke sharply to a blue puddle of moonlight and a smell that he thought at first was roses. For a moment he thought Lark had come after all. There had always been a smell of roses around her. Sometimes that was the only way he had known she was there. But it was Norah, sitting on his bed beside him, wearing the red dressing-gown that had gone bald with washing. The smell was not roses but Imperial Leather soap and clean hair.

It was a relief to see her familiar bulk, outlined in silver by the moon. He wanted her to be there forever. She anchored him to the world as no one else had ever done. Between them, in their different ways, Lark and Norah had saved his life. He wasn't sure he could manage alone.

'You were dreaming,' she said, softly. 'A bad dream.'

'I don't remember dreaming anything,' he said truthfully, when he had pulled himself together enough to speak. 'I hope I wasn't making a horrible siren noise, like Errol.'

'No,' she assured him, in a throaty whisper. 'I just came in to see you before I went to bed. I had you on my mind. I wanted to tell you I'm sure you've made the right decision. They really do want you, Gerry. It's not what you're afraid of — that they just feel guilty about you. Although obviously they do and with good reason, too. But there's a lot more to their feelings about

24

bringing you back into the family than that. They *are* your family and they need you with them, very badly. I want you to hang on to that because I know at first things won't be easy for you and – well, I don't want you to panic. It won't just be one-sided. Honestly. You need each other.'

'I was doing all right here,' he said, with a flash of rebellion. 'If you really want to know, Norah, just at this moment I feel as if I need all this like a hole in the head.' *Hole in the heart*, he thought.

'Sssh – You'll wake the little spaceman over there.' She nodded towards the restless sighing mound in the other bed where Errol was uneasily asleep with Gerard's birthday earphones on. 'Yes – I know you were happy in a funny kind of way, not asking for much, just hibernating, waiting till you're quite sure winter's over. But underneath, all the same, I think you've been secretly longing for people of your own – and I believe there are people in your family who long for you in the same way. Even if they don't know it yet.'

He didn't like the sound of this at all. 'If I'm not wanted there, I'll hike straight back here to Deben House,' he said fiercely. 'Thank you very much.'

She smiled at him then, a lopsided beautiful smile which utterly transformed her blunt, battered face. It was as if she had touched him. As if she knew him through and through and really liked what she knew. He understood that whatever happened Norah would always be on his side. The aching knot that had been forming inside, using up most of the space where his heart and lungs should be, slowly dissolved. Without knowing it he had been partially holding his breath for a long time. Now he found himself letting it go in a sigh of relief. He would survive, her smile promised him.

'Goodnight then, Gerry,' she said, briefly patting the quilt beside his hand, her dry fingers brushing his, and then, only staying long enough to remove Gerard's earphones gently from Errol's head, she left the room. And this leavetaking, the private, almost wordless one in the middle of the night, was the real one, as far as Gerard was concerned.

Saying goodbye to everyone else a few hours later by daylight was every bit as bad as Gerard had known it would be. Worse in fact. Worst of all was leaving Errol who bolted upstairs at the last moment, and shut himself in their bedroom howling like a puppy that knows it's going to be drowned. He wouldn't come down however hard they pleaded. In the end some of the girls burst out crying too.

Steven smirked away like mad and went beetroot red to match his ears. But Jason just gave Gerard a hard look through his double strength spectacles and said mysteriously, 'You must never stop believing in the Future Rose.' Or did he say Future Road? Either way it was, like all Jason's utterances, completely incomprehensible.

But as he stood clutching Jason's own beloved and much read copy of *Green Slime*, watching his friend wander off into the back garden alone, skreeping and groking, his hands in his pockets, his shoulders hunched up so far they were almost level with his ears, he realised he was going to miss Jason.

Somewhere near the door his uncle stood, waiting. But Gerard was afraid to look at him while the goodbyes were still going on. He felt himself to be a small anonymous rock at the sea's edge, while all around him his old familiar and his strange new lives went surging in and out of each other like the mingling colours and temperatures of incoming and outgoing tides.

He was deeply afraid, though whether of being overwhelmed with some terrifying new ecstasy or appallingly cheated and let down, he didn't know.

He was lying to himself. He did know. Secretly, underneath he knew all the time what he longed for. But he was ashamed of his fantasy. The giddy rush of joy, of knowing and being known, *coming home*.

Oh it was all right, he knew it would never happen. Why else did they make all those endless soft focus commercials: the wide unfriendly winter world shut safely outside the curtains, while you sat blissful by the fire drinking cream of leek soup with all your loved ones. He wasn't the only displaced person in the world hopefully gulping down cream of leek soup by the pint.

At last, hearing Norah say something and realising she was speaking encouragingly to him, he lifted up his eyes to look properly at Uncle Avery for the first time. And then he knew how right he was to squelch his pathetic fantasies before they'd had the chance to take him over.

Because his uncle was very tall, Gerard's eyes had to travel up a considerable length of smooth grey-silver suiting before they reached his face, finding that this too was shaved satin-smooth behind gold wire glasses. So here was Uncle Avery.

But where, exactly, was he?

Everywhere Gerard looked, Uncle Avery presented

gleaming, impeccably groomed surfaces. But the surfaces led nowhere. Like messages carefully preserved and buried for future generations, they seemed impermeably sealed. There was no way in to Uncle Avery. Gerard's tentative smile of greeting bounced off him as though intercepted by radar. Uncle Avery himself was smiling but the smile was neutral, strictly functional.

And then he was shaking Gerard's sweating, nervous hand with his own cool impersonal hand that smelled faintly of sandalwood soap and he said, across Siberian wasteland, 'Well, Gerard – you aren't as large as I thought you would be for fourteen. But then Lindsey was always a little half-grown mouse of a thing. Are you ready? Have you packed up all your worldly goods, young man?'

Gerard was in fact standing beside the worldly goods referred to; two whole cases full of them and a couple of bulging carrier bags. Perhaps it didn't look like much to Uncle Avery. The wicket-keeping gloves were in one of the carriers. Norah had remembered after all. They were brilliant: the best ones in the sports catalogue.

He looked around at everyone for one last time. He was praying that he wouldn't panic and disgrace Norah at the last minute. With every fibre of his being he longed to hurl himself into her sensible, scratchy grey flannel lap and howl like a fourteen-year-old Errol: 'No! Don't make me! I don't want to!'

But with a massive internal struggle, equivalent to an ocean liner turning itself around in mid-Atlantic, he only said, 'Yes thank you. I'm quite ready, thank you.'

And somehow he was hugging Norah and Phil and Mrs Grist. Somehow he was saying goodbye to the only people in the world that he knew and loved, but even so, not really his people. And he was climbing dazed into his uncle's sleek silver Mercedes and fastening his safety belt and the car was pulling away and he thought it must, it really must all be a dream. It didn't help that his real self had flown away as it always did on such occasions, wilfully leaving behind only a vague ghostly Gerard to travel with the uncle who was his real family yet a total stranger: his private thoughts and feelings as carefully locked away from his nephew as the invisible contents of Uncle Avery's expensive calfskin briefcase.

3

The Alchemist's House

In Gerard's wide experience of dreadful journeys the journey to Owlcote was a journey of unparalleled dreadfulness. And it was no help to him to realise that Uncle Avery found it every bit as unnerving.

It's my fault, Gerard thought drearily. It's me.

And he began to be convinced that in the company of a more articulate, less panic-stricken nephew, Uncle Avery would be transformed into an entirely different relation.

As it was, they passed the hours in mutual suffering. At first his uncle tried to talk to him in a jovial interviewing sort of way, asking him how well he was getting on at school and what his 'interests' were. Gerard lied a bit about school in the hope that the lies might miraculously turn out to be truths in the context of his brave new life but decided not to tell Uncle Avery how much he enjoyed making omelettes and chocolate mousse.

But when they had drained this meagre supply of conversation painfully dry, the silences grew longer and deeper as if they fattened on embarrassment. Occasionally his uncle fired facts at him, perhaps in the hope of remedying what Gerard knew to be a sadly defective education. The facts were apparently generated in response to whatever scenery they were passing through at the time. In this way Gerard learned more about the Iceni than he really wanted to and certainly more about the feudal strip field farming system than he thought he would ever need to use.

Gerard learned that Uncle Avery had read history at university before he changed to law. Nowadays he ran the family's solicitor's practice in Stamford in Lincolnshire.

After a while, no doubt bored by the dullness of Gerard's responses, his uncle switched on the radio and for the next hour or so the silver Mercedes floated like a sealed spacecraft through rainswept Suffolk villages he could neither hear nor smell nor touch: all to the remote sweet strains of some kind of classical music. It wasn't that he didn't like the car or the music. He loved the car, though it filled him with awe. Secretly he would have liked to stroke the upholstery. If he had felt for one moment that he had the right to be here, he would have liked to ask his uncle how everything worked. And he might even have liked the music very much if only there had been some part of it that he could get hold of and recognise and name or hum.

Eventually a news programme replaced the music and the rain eased off. Uncle Avery switched off the wipers. When they stopped for a hamburger at a roadside restaurant, the clouds were already rolling away.

Gerard wasn't actually very fond of hamburgers though as his uncle ordered two for him, he accepted them and, when they were brought, politely tucked in. But he guessed that Uncle Avery, travelling alone, would have chosen a different place, offering different food.

When his uncle's own meal arrived he managed a few mouthfuls but then pushed it irritably aside and instead drank two cups of black coffee. And all the while they were in the restaurant, he edgily tapped his fingers as if involuntarily enduring a second, but this time internal, radio concert.

To his own surprise Gerard enjoyed his hamburgers. Food always cheered him up, though he preferred good food. And he adored the enormous freezing cold Coke his uncle ordered for him. It filled him full of fizz. He could feel it lapping buoyantly at the insides of his ears.

Before they left he managed to slide some sugar cubes off the table into his pockets, in case of meeting horses later. Even imagining that he might, made him feel oddly more hopeful and at the same time rather less ghostly and less tongue-tied. So when they started off again down the A1, he tried to talk to Uncle Avery about cricket and what had happened last season when England played Pakistan and, so his uncle wouldn't think he was a complete moron, he even started to describe a book he'd just finished called *The Final Test*. But Uncle Avery never read novels and he wasn't interested in cricket, though he told Gerard grudgingly that there was a local cricket club he could perhaps try out for – 'if your grandmother doesn't object.'

This was the first mention Gerard had heard of a grandmother and he felt an immediate stab of anxiety. For some reason this old woman had the power to interfere just as much as she chose in other people's lives. Even in matters that couldn't remotely concern her, like whether other people played cricket or not.

Images of Norah rose up unbidden. He drove them

away sternly. She had done all she could. Now it was up to him.

'I do like your car,' he said. 'It's the poshest car I've ever been in in all my life.' He grinned hopefully, sure that his uncle too must love this sleek enigmatic silver goddess since he had chosen her, wondering if this of all topics might be the one which would crack Uncle Avery's secret combination.

But Uncle Avery said only in his light, toneless voice that the insurance on a Mercedes was crippling and the servicing charges equally prohibitive.

Baffled and uneasy, Gerard thought it must be depressing to be so tantalisingly surrounded by all kinds of lovely pleasures and luxuries yet utterly incapable, for some perplexing reason, to relax and enjoy any of them. Personally he'd had more actual fun on a windy day out at Minsmere with Norah in her ancient Renault 4, with only a packet of Mrs Grist's cheese and pickle sandwiches between them.

'Have you explained to my cousins all about me?' he asked at last. What he really longed for, what he had secretly longed for from the beginning, was for his uncle to talk to him about his own mother, Lindsey. But somehow this had become less and less possible as the journey went on. From the start there had been this ghastly frigid atmosphere, as though Avery experienced the return of his nephew not so much as a homecoming, as the coming of some kind of doom.

'Well the twins are rather young to understand everything that's involved,' said his uncle guardedly. 'But Harriet knows all about you, yes.'

From his uncle's tone Gerard suspected that Harriet might perhaps not be too thrilled. Probably she had been as shocked to hear of his existence as he had to learn he had a whole lost family. He didn't much like her name. He imagined her saying it with a slight sneer. 'I'm Harriet.' He could just picture her with ash blonde hair all down her snooty back and a cool blue stare and a superior horsey voice.

'Does Harriet have a horse?' he asked after a while. His fantasy had supplied her already with jodphurs and riding boots, a silly horse-riding hat. He liked horses but despised the sort of people he imagined to ride them.

His uncle snorted, actually laughing for the first time, though it was a swallowed-down sort of laugh with little amusement in it. 'Might do her a bit of good if she did,' he said. 'But no, Gerard, I'm afraid she hasn't. She's afraid of horses as it happens. Always has been. She rather likes dogs, I think,' he added, 'but of course we can't have one because of the twins' allergies. She used to have an imaginary dog for a while when she was small.'

An imaginary dog. Good grief.

'That's a shame,' said Gerard aloud, seizing these unexpected puzzle pieces and squirrelling them away like the sugar lumps, for later.

His uncle gave him a quick doubting sideways glance and then went back to concentrating on the road which had gradually become narrower and more winding and was twisting at this moment through a small attractive village: cottages of soft golden stone bordering a village green, a river flowing under a low stone bridge.

Suddenly, as Gerard looked with delight at this serene golden country scene, there was a beating of agitated wings inside him and, inexplicably, reality divided itself

34

so that he seemed somehow to perceive a second, darker, less coherent scene, filtered through the sunlit layer of the first.

Gold, he thought involuntarily. Curse.

Shove off, Lark, he warned. *Not now, all right.* She really knew how to pick her moments.

Then the sunlit afternoon brightened, solidified again and the queasy sensation of being split into two, left him as though it had never been.

Had Lark really done that? It was the weirdest thing he had ever seen her do, if so. If he had actually seen anything, that is. He was already beginning to doubt what he'd experienced. He thought he was probably a bit carsick after the long journey.

'People can't always have what they want,' said Uncle Avery, apparently pursuing old grievances of his own. 'If she had a dog I'm sure she'd soon discover her parents had always deprived her of something else.'

'Earth, Fire, Water, Air,' sang the thin sad voice. 'Met together in a garden fair.'

Gerard swallowed hard and stayed silent for several reasons.

He had meant it was a shame about the allergies, not about the dog. There was a girl at Norah's once who was allergic to things. It was her private language of unhappiness. Instead of stealing or screaming or telling lies or hitting out, she scrawled her rage and fear all over her own body in burning scarlet braille.

'Nearly there now, young man,' said his uncle frigidly after a while.

Now they were getting closer to Owlcote, Uncle Avery seemed compelled to be educational again. He made a stiff little speech about what an ancient family the Noones were, then launched into a confused and confusing history concerning Thomas Noone, the ancestor who had built Owlcote; a perfect specimen of Elizabethan Man, Avery said. A man of science as well of the arts. Able to turn his hand to anything and everything. Uncle Avery talked of this long-since perished marvel as though he had personally known and admired him and his awesome ability to live out his dreams on such a grand scale.

It was the first time his uncle had shown any sign of enthusiasm. It was almost as though Avery would like to have had a shot at being an Elizabethan Noone, Gerard thought vaguely, only half able to listen, busy as he was, struggling to subdue his own increasingly panic-stricken insides. As though Avery actually envied his ancestor and would have swapped twentieth-century plumbing and penicillin in a trice just to have the world still so green and new, not yet shrunken down like a cheap sweater. Of course, Avery went on, Thomas Noone had had his sorrows . . .

Gerard tensed, glimpsing distant towers amongst leafy green. Suddenly the road was achingly familiar.

'Even dabbled in alchemy at one time,' his uncle was saying. 'But of course he recognised it as the pseudo science it was and locked up the room he had used for his laboratory and, legend has it, threw away the key.' He glanced at Gerard and mistaking his carefully blank expression for ignorance said too patiently, 'Alchemy. Turning base metals into gold.' Swallowing, Gerard nodded.

A signpost warned of a concealed entrance ahead.

'This is it,' said his uncle.

Gerard's heart thudded.

Uncle Avery drove carefully up a long, meandering private drive and pulled up alongside some mossy looking outbuildings that served as garages.

When the engine was switched off the country silence was so absolute that Gerard was deafened by the lonely beating of his own blood inside his ears.

He was home! He knew it.

I've been telling you, said Lark. *It's been waiting for you all the time.*

They were climbing out of the car. The sun shone through fine April rain; confusing weather that expressed Gerard's own confusion perfectly.

'This way,' said his uncle.

In the cropped turf, ranks of daffodils bowed stiff yellow frills, their new unused looking blooms streaked like unripe fruit with pallid green. Gerard touched the drooping bud of one. It was cold. Rainwater spilled out of it, soaking his cuff.

They skirted a high curving wall of mellow golden stone over which Gerard glimpsed the pale blossoming boughs of an orchard. Again something stirred in his heart.

This is my home.

Then he thought: and someone's watching me.

'The orchard,' said his uncle, austerely. 'But no apple scrumping for you, young man, later in the year.'

They arrived at a great iron gate with some ancient heraldic emblem blazoned above it. Gerard was too panicked, too full of conflicting emotions to take in anything but the vaguest impression of some fire-producing serpent or dragon-like creature.

Beside the gate, as though guarding it, was a tall and twisted lilac tree of such great age that its grey contorted roots had grown through the wall, becoming a living part of it. Just as Gerard was about to follow his uncle through the gate into the garden beyond, the air stirred with a vigorous breeze and the warm light perfume of flowering lilacs enveloped him so powerfully and personally that it was as startling to Gerard as if the tree had cried out his name aloud.

Shaken, he looked up just as a cascade of petals showered upon his head and shoulders like a blessing.

Secretly crouching, watching their arrival from her hiding place in the old summer house, Harriet saw. She knew the lilac tree had not been long in flower. She knew that until that precise moment the day had been still. She knew there was no scientific or common sense reason for lilac blossoms to loosen themselves and descend upon the dull and mousy head of her cousin. And she saw Gerard's startled glance upwards and how he almost laughed aloud, but stopped himself, hastily following her father through the gate so as not to be left behind.

Perhaps he's the one, she thought. Even though he looks worse than useless. All small and pinched in that ghastly mud-coloured anorak. But if it isn't him it's all hopeless. He's the last chance. My very last chance.

4

Distant Cousins

'Your aunt Caroline and the children and I live in the west wing,' said Uncle Avery, apparently unconscious of sounding like a character in an old film. 'Mother lives in a separate part of the house with her own companion-housekeeper. You'll find that she is a very independent-minded woman. Your uncle William runs his own small business from Owlcote and has a flat over the old stables.'

He was striding ahead of Gerard now, a moving column of silver and grey, and Gerard, trying to keep up as well as he could, felt quite dazed at the proximity of so many new relations. Hadn't anyone in this house, apart from his own mother, ever grown up and left home?

'Perhaps it seems very glamorous to you to live in a grand old house like this, but I can assure you that it costs a sizable fortune just to keep it standing. And I'm afraid Mother doesn't – '

He never finished telling Gerard what his mother didn't do for at this moment two little fair-haired children in identical denim dungarees and red wellington boots, burst out of a concealed side door, shrieking and giggling and shoving at each other in their excitement.

Behind them came Aunt Caroline, wearing the same soft flowery dress she had worn in the photograph. She looked almost as excited as the twins.

'Gerard,' she cried, and her voice surprised him with a throaty carrying power that contradicted the harmless floweriness of the rest of her. 'How wonderful that you're actually here at last! Is it all right to hug you? Oh there's so much for us all to talk about – I shan't know where to begin. We've all got such a lot of catching up to – '

'Don't overwhelm the boy,' said Uncle Avery, just as Gerard, shyly but happily, went forward to let himself be embraced. Suddenly flushing and awkward, Aunt Caroline dropped her arms to her sides and gave him a clumsy pat on the shoulder instead of a hug, leaving him adrift in a swirl of raw emotions.

Feeling somehow stranded between the rather intense warmth of his aunt and the polar hostility of his uncle, he was reminded of winter evenings at one foster home, when, awarded the wrong end of the sofa, he found himself suffering the rival claims of a coal fire so ardent it melted the marrow out of one half of him, and a window so draughty that the other half froze all to liver-dappled marble, like a Victorian mantelpiece.

'She's made a HUGE chocolate cake for you,' said one of the twins, 'but I can't eat it because I'm allergic to chocolate. So's Flora.'

Gerard noticed now that the little boy's face was covered with small scaly patches like burns.

'Oh you,' scolded Aunt Caroline. 'I made something else special for you, you little fraud. I always do. You know I do.'

'Carob cookies – Yuk!' said the other twin. 'You needn't bother.' She grinned at Gerard, out of angelic pale blue eyes, showing tiny pearly white teeth. 'Carob cookies stink.'

'Oh come in – come in,' cried poor Aunt Caroline. 'Don't let's keep Gerard standing out in the cold and wet. Let him come into his new home. I'm afraid I don't know where Harriet has gone. She went flying off somewhere hours ago. She's rather a law unto herself, Gerard, as you'll soon discover.'

At this, Uncle Avery's face did not so much change as invisibly tighten upon itself, and his breathing became abruptly harsh and rapid as though it would have liked to spurt out of his nostrils in fiery clouds.

But all he said in his toneless voice was, 'Harriet knows she should be here. There isn't any excuse for that kind of rudeness. You're always too soft with her, Carrie.'

And he stalked past them into the house.

'Oh she didn't mean to be rude,' said Gerard's aunt, trying to smile, 'it's just that she's a bit shy about meeting people. It's a funny age fourteen, isn't it?'

Gerard guessed she hadn't wanted the first moments of the reunion to go quite like this. She had put her faith in the healing powers of hugs and tears and chocolate cake. 'I haven't been it for very long myself, so I can't exactly tell it from being thirteen yet.'

'Oh Gerard,' said his aunt in anguish, 'you're the same age of course. It's just that you're not as – that I'd completely forgotten. I've got the tact of a bulldozer. Oh do stop giggling, twins. They think everything is so funny. Gerard, come in, come in.'

Then, as they went into the house, she actually managed to give him a brief nervous hug, banging Gerard's head in their mutual confusion and making his ears ring but otherwise cheering him up enormously.

'Gerard,' she said. 'If you knew how I wish – '

But then she changed her mind about whatever she was going to say, crying out instead in a bright voice, 'Come into the kitchen, because it's the one room in this old house one can depend upon to be cosy. It really is the heart of the house now we've finally got our Aga. I'll make us all a pot of tea and you can recover from your awful journey. I always used to feel so dreadfully sick in cars when I was your age.'

'He's not one of the twins, you know,' said Uncle Avery, leaning over the sink heavily, swallowing a second white tablet, 'so you don't have to talk to him as if he's four.'

'Avery — one of your heads. I am sorry.' Aunt Caroline flew to him and laid an anxious hand upon his sleeve as though she believed herself personally responsible.

'It was a long drive,' said Uncle Avery, via Cape Canaveral. 'I'm going to catch up with some work.'

And without another word he left the kitchen. Later, at a little distance, Gerard heard a door slam.

Gerard understood, as he was clearly meant to, that his uncle, by unwillingly giving up part of a working day to collect his disappointing nephew, had given himself an attack of migraine. It didn't make him feel very comfortable, but he discovered with a sense of relief that he didn't actually feel particularly guilty. It seemed to him that Uncle Avery derived a great deal of unhealthy satisfaction from making people feel continually guilty or in the wrong. If you were going to be one of his official dependents you'd be expected to pay the price in a regular guilt tithe.

Gerard decided that for now at any rate, he would concentrate on getting to know his aunt. She shouldn't let everyone push her around so much, he thought. She could do with toughening-up lessons from Norah.

But she did make the most tremendous chocolate cake, he discovered, his mouth full.

'Your kitchen is huge,' he said, crumbily.

The twins hung around, breathing heavily and swinging on the furniture, waiting for their cousin to get interesting enough to justify the excitement of his arrival.

'Stop it, Laurie. Stop scraping that chair and *don't* hover over poor Gerard like that, Flora, you'll make him nervous. Yes, isn't it enormous. It was absolutely dreadful before we got the Aga. A great dreary barn. Not a real family kitchen at all. But now it's alive and it feels like my own kingdom. I love it. I just wish we could bring all of Owlcote alive like this.'

'You must really like to cook.'

He eyed the bunches of herbs hanging from beams, jostling fading dried flowers and long strings of onions and garlic. 'Brilliant lot of knives,' he added, spotting a vicious looking battery of cooking knives of all shapes and sizes. Beside the door he noticed wellingtons caked with mud, a muddy trowel and a pair of secateurs in a basket.

'I was gardening for a bit, this morning,' she said following his gaze. 'You have to dodge the showers and get out when you can, this time of year. There's such a lot to be done. That's my other kingdom out there. Actually I'd love to get my hands on all the gardens at Owlcote but for the time being I have to be satisfied with my vegetable patch. Can't you just imagine how different it must all have looked when the house was first built?'

'I don't know anything about old houses and gardens,' he said shyly. 'Wouldn't it have been much the same? Flowers and trees and things?'

'Oh no, Gerard. The ancestor of yours who built the house during Elizabeth's reign – Thomas Noone – he was a real powerhouse of energy, fascinated by everything, turned his hand to anything. So when he designed the gardens it wasn't enough for them to be just pleasant green spaces, you see, though there would have been a few of those too. Elizabethans weren't terribly interested in imitating Nature. Nature was only a starting point – raw material to be improved on by Art. So Thomas Noone's garden would have been full of contrivances and clever devices and hidden meanings – a work of art just like a painting or a poem, but a living one, one you could walk through and amuse yourself in. Have you ever heard of knot gardens?' She drew a deep breath. 'I'd love to recreate an Elizabethan knot garden with all the right sixteenth-century plants, the proper coloured sands and gravels. I won't try to describe one to you, I'll find you a picture of one in one of my books. Maybe you could even help me make one, one day – Oh, Gerard, you should stop me or I just go on and on,' she said, suddenly interrupting herself, looking dismayed. 'Why ever should I imagine you'd be interested in gardening. Young people never are, are they? I'm sure I never was. It's one of those things that overtakes you like grey hairs or fallen arches. Tell me what sort of things you like doing?'

She looked genuinely distressed. She really went in for guilt in a big way, Gerard thought. He liked it best when she let herself be carried away by her own enthusiasm instead of feeling single-handedly responsible for his happiness. When people felt obliged to wear themselves out making you happy, you felt equally exhaustingly obliged to be in a permanent state of euphoria just to put their minds at rest.

'I wasn't bored, you know,' he said frankly to set her straight. 'I was enjoying listening. I'm not actually good at very much, I'm afraid. Except cricket. But sometimes Norah used to let me cook and I got quite good at that. I made a soufflé once. We watched it rise in Mrs Grist's new fan oven with the glass door. Mrs Grist said it was better than the telly. Then we ate it with salad. It looked better than it tasted actually. It was just like eating posh scrambled eggs. But it was fun making it and watching it all puff up.' He laughed, remembering it.

'I'm sorry my uncle's got a headache because of me, Aunt Caroline,' he added to his own surprise. 'Do you think he'd feel better if someone took him a cup of tea?'

'Please just call me Caroline,' she said. 'Then perhaps I won't feel quite so nervous. Your uncle is under a lot of strain at the moment. He has an awful lot of responsibility – keeping up this place is almost a full-time job in itself, and then he has to work so hard at the office, and his mother isn't terribly well just now. You really mustn't think it's anything to do with you.'

She bit her lip, an unconscious habit that was already growing familiar to Gerard.

For a moment he saw her with extraordinary vividness as she must have been at his own age, lonely, awkward in school uniform (posh uniform, he thought), biting her lip, her eyes lowered, promising to do better, her best never good enough.

'Could I see my – could I see where I'm supposed to

put my things?' he asked, realising he didn't actually know what plans had been made for his arrival. He quite fancied seeing the rest of the house. He'd only caught a glimpse as he came into the kitchen; a wide hall with glowing rugs laid over polished wood, and a broad curving stairway with beautiful carved bannisters.

'Of course you'll want to see your room. What am I thinking of! Though I'm not terribly happy about it, to be honest. We had to throw things together in rather a hurry. But perhaps when it's all more settled we can make better arrangements for you. It was Will's idea, actually. He seemed to think – ' she faltered, then rushed on, 'but I wasn't terribly sure – well I'm sure it could be a pretty room, but I'm afraid we haven't managed to get round to decorating it and it is an attic room, Gerard, so it might be rather cold. I lit a fire to welcome you but I think the chimney might need – '

'It'll be a luxury just having a room all to myself,' he interrupted, feeling quite battered by her concern for him. It was like being forced through some kind of emotional car wash. 'I'll love it,' he reassured her. 'You've no idea. I've always shared with two or three other people before. Jonathon went home last month, though, so then there was just me and Errol. But Errol had very noisy night terrors so I always had to have a supply of Polos handy to shut him up.'

He had hoped to cheer Caroline up and take her mind off the latest instalment of the guilt tax, but his innocent mention of everyday life at Deben House only seemed to make things worse.

'Oh, Gerard,' she said. 'I do feel so ashamed of us all. All those years of being on your own. How can we ever

46

– ' She bit her lip again and when a twin came to tug at her skirt she said irritably, 'Oh, Laurie, whatever is it now?'

Which fortunately stopped Gerard from risking the question that welled from his heart and seemed to dam up behind his throat like swallowed-down tears.

Why now? Why did you suddenly try to find me after all this time? It was a question that felt too dangerous. Like a dark well he might stumble into and drown.

Instead he said as cheerfully as he could, 'Tell me where the room is. I'll find it. If I don't come back by supper time, send out the twins with brandy barrels.'

Long ago he had discovered that if you made people laugh, it made them feel more at home with you. It was easier then for them to like you.

When Caroline smiled, he let his breath go with relief. It would have been too soon to ask why they had suddenly decided they wanted him. He might not even be staying that long.

She gave directions and Gerard set off, wishing he hadn't reminded himself that his morning had begun a hundred years ago with Errol screaming and howling in their old shared room. He felt a louse, leaving the little boy all alone to brave the spooks and vampires.

Owlcote had been designed by Thomas Noone in the shape of a gigantic capital letter E, in celebration, Uncle Avery had told him, of his ruling sovereign. Each projecting corner had its tower rooms, symmetrically balancing one another. Apparently the Elizabethans were hot on symmetry.

Gerard's attic was in the tower at the back of the west wing. With the growing feeling that his life had turned into some kind of fairy-tale he started up the

47

stairs. After the glowing warmth of his aunt's kitchen, the upper storeys had a dank chilly feel. The twins shared a room on the same floor as their parents. Harriet's room was on the next floor up. Gerard's was even closer to the sky.

The tower stairs were clammy and so narrow he felt them press in unpleasantly upon him. The wood was worn and worm-eaten. As he climbed further and further away from the warm, lived-in, part of the house, his confidence ebbed with his body heat. Once again he found himself in a house where he didn't properly belong. He had sworn it would never happen again and things really had been different for a time at Norah's. He thought he had beaten it. Sometimes, he thought, living was pretty much like being stuck in a revolving door. Same old scenery, same old situations, coming round again and again.

Then he thought of the amazing, ridiculous coincidence of the welcoming lilac tree and took heart. Perhaps one day he might belong again. It was bound to take time. That was what Norah had wanted him to understand, that last night.

He was still toiling up stairs. Now and again he passed windows, set curiously low down in the wall: narrow barred lozenges of light, giving a glimpse of soft damp greenery, budding trees, daffodils.

At last after the final corkscrew twist he found a low door, not much higher than himself and pushed it open into a surprisingly large round room, rather bare of furniture but full of a sad fading light and the soft lament of doves. For a fleeting heartbeat of a moment he thought he saw someone curled up on the window seat, a small dark animal beside her. But it was only a trick of the light, shadows thrown by a tall old-fashioned oak chest.

He stood quite still, surveying his attic room. The most interesting thing in it, apart from the window seat, was a very ancient-looking carved cupboard set into the wall beside his bed. He opened it but it was empty except for a little dust. Apart from this there was a wardrobe for his clothes, some old faded carpet with a great deal of bare floorboard around it, some book-shelves with a few old paperbacks propped up at one end, and a rather muddled-looking corner stacked with old tin trunks and boxes which Aunt Caroline hadn't yet had time to find another home for.

He closed the door behind him. Someone had left a bunch of wild flowers on his bed. First primroses, he thought, wondering who could have left them for him. He picked them up by their damp pink stalks, burying his face in pale blooms and fleshy leaves, breathing them in.

They smelled mossy and secretive. He imagined for a moment that he felt a faint wild pulse, as if he held spring itself, like a fallen bird, in his hands. He put them down.

They're just flowers he thought. Grow up.

On one wall was a hooded stone fireplace with a rough-hewn primitive look to it. Caroline was quite right to suspect the condition of the chimney. It was the most cheerless and inadequate fire imaginable. It was simply not true, he thought, that there was no smoke without fire.

He moved closer to the hearth, shivering, trying to warm himself amongst the billowing yellowish clouds. She was right to feel guilty. She deserved to feel bad about it. It was a dismal apology for a room. It was old and cold. It felt soaked with loneliness as if it had been occupied by a dreary succession of despairing exiles.

Suddenly he felt desperate. He needed Lark. There was always light and warmth where Lark was. Light and the smell of summer roses. She had a shining knot at her throat. She was always fiddling with it. It was the most vivid thing about her. The rest was always faded, both sepia and silvery, like a shadow that had made up its mind to become real. He had called her out of the shadows, as a magician might call a spirit out of a stone.

After that he had never again been a prisoner inside himself, whatever they did to him. Between them Lark and Gerard had the doors to all the worlds.

I know, I know, he told her silently. You choose your own times and seasons and all that enigmatic stuff. But I'm not sure I can manage this alone. I know you're around so you might as well talk to me. Was it you that did the primroses?

No, she said, stirring at last, to his relief, adding inexplicably, *That was Alice. She's been waiting for you. Have you got the Gift?*

Her silly idea of a joke. Did she still think he was six?

He did have it actually. His fingers closed over the little carved bobbin in his pocket. It fitted exactly into his palm, rounded and worn, like driftwood that is pounded and bleached into satin smoothness by the waves.

'Yes,' he assented, sighing. 'If it makes you feel better.'

Alice likes you, she commented. *She thinks you might be the one.*

This was ridiculous. He couldn't get a sensible word out of her.

'Who on earth's Alice?' he said impatiently, out loud. 'Is that another cousin?' Flaming hell, he thought, I hope not.

Distantly, said Lark elusively. *I suppose.*

'I want you to talk to me properly again,' Gerard burst out angrily. 'Like you used to. Not in hints and riddles. If you're going to keep hanging around I want to be able to see you, like I did before.'

But there was no gauzy disturbance of air: no girl of sepia and faded silver. Only smudges of smoke hanging in the clammy air.

'*Earth, Fire, Water, Air. Met together in a garden fair –*'

Gerard frowned. There was that queasy dislocated feeling that he had first experienced in the car. Who had spoken? Not spoken, chanted: half singing. Not Lark, he knew. Had the voice been inside his head, or outside in his room? Riddling nonsense words, that made his skin prickle and his stomach churn. Why were they so familiar?

Lark apparently felt sorry for him now.

It's too soon, she said, pityingly. *Much too soon. Go over to your window and look out and tell me what you can see.*

He was unwilling to humour her. He was angry with her but he was frightened too. It was as if she was drifting further and further beyond his reach, only half with him even now, and fading fast. There was something hasty and last minute about her most recent intrusions, like shouted reminders as a train pulls away from the station – Don't forget to write, take your vitamins, wash behind your ears. Remember me –

Lark was the one fixed point of his life. The one

person who really knew him, who had been through the dark days and shared his fears and longings. She was impossible when she insisted on turning up at the wrong time. But if she left him now he didn't think he could stand it. Not another leavetaking.

He did what she asked. He knelt up on the window seat and eventually succeeded in pushing open the leaded window. A pair of white birds fluttered up from a nearby sill, alarmed. Doves imported by Caroline for Thomas Noone's dovecote.

He was looking down over wet green parkland in the gathering dusk. For the first time he saw the glittering serpentine curve of the river. The pale blur of blossom must be the back of the orchard. And at some distance from the house itself a peculiar formation of high straggling box hedges which apparently served no practical purpose at all.

He leaned out dangerously, peering with screwed-up eyes to try to see if he could make out what it might be, feeling all at once pulled towards it by a powerful yearning. It was like not knowing he was thirsty until someone offered him water. His throat contracted, parched, aching; but for what?

Something was waiting there. Something or someone, calling him.

In the morning he could go down and explore, he thought. But it was time Lark answered some questions. He shouldn't let her get away with it. His life was upside down and inside out and somehow, he just knew Lark was in it up to her neck. She had been his friend, imaginary or not. She owed him answers. 'Lark,' he began –

But as he turned back into the darkening room he

saw in the doorway, to his dismay, a tall round-shouldered brown-skinned girl in glasses.

'Do you always talk to yourself?' she asked unpleasantly. 'I expect you've guessed I'm Harriet. I wanted to introduce myself, that's why I kept out of the way. Anything to avoid having to endure my mother and father talking patronisingly over the top of my head, explaining me. We can't talk now, I'm afraid. We're all summoned to Granny Noone's in your honour. But you've got to promise to meet me later, when we can. It's absolutely life and death. Promise?' She clenched her fists in their black woollen gloves as she spoke and Gerard thought she'd probably hit him if he refused.

'What about "Hallo"?' he asked, taken aback. She had the posh accent all right but he couldn't have been more mistaken about everything else.

'Oh I don't care about superficial rubbish like that,' said Harriet stonily. 'I care about the things that matter. I hoped you would too.'

She glowered at him as if she had already made up her mind that he would disappoint her. 'Well, you'd better follow me,' she flung at him. 'You don't stand a hope in hell of finding it by yourself.'

Then she flew away down the tower staircase.

'And if you aren't just a wimp,' she said, apparently through clenched teeth, as they both pounded down and around the twisting stairs, 'I'll meet you down by the river at ten tomorrow morning. By the old boathouse.'

'I'm sorry,' puffed Gerard, feeling he must have missed something. 'Aren't we going to be living in the same house? Do we need to be quite so cloak and dagger about it?'

'Yes, if you really have to have it spelled out, we do,'

she said as though to an idiot. 'Because I don't want them to know we've exchanged so much as one civil word, okay?'

Not much danger of that, thought Gerard, almost wanting to laugh. Not so far, anyway. 'I see,' he said, untruthfully. 'Well, that's a relief. I was beginning to think that perhaps people in your family always had to make appointments to meet each other.'

As he had expected from the start, he didn't like his cousin at all, yet he was intrigued by her despite himself and he didn't want to let her get away with too much. She could keep her snooty superiority to herself. But without deigning to reply, Harriet flew off along a corridor lined with the kind of paintings he had only ever seen in stately homes. Artificial compositions of sombre-looking people in dark, stiff clothing, with hounds at their feet and falcons on their wrists and the children, like stern miniature adults, with swords for the boys and pearl necklaces for the girls.

Coo, thought a dazed Gerard. My flipping ancestors. I don't believe this.

He followed his cousin down a short curving flight of stairs ornamented with intricate wood carvings, through an arching oak door that reminded him of churches, down another passage and into a suddenly dense and unpleasant cooking smell, immediately identified by Gerard's flaring nostrils as 'School Dinners'.

'Mrs Krake's cabbage,' Harriet remarked over her shoulder. 'Hold your breath.'

Through a half-open door, Gerard, valiantly holding his breath as advised, caught a glimpse of the person he supposed to be Mrs Krake amidst steaming pans in a sinister cupboard of a kitchen. He thought there was something rather grand and contemptuous about the way she went on slamming things about without so much as a curious glance at them as they charged past.

Harriet ran fast and easily on her long muscular legs but she carried her head strangely low, her shoulders hunched as if to take up less space or perhaps to make herself less visible.

From close-up he saw she had quite a large quantity of hair but, rather perversely, he thought, she had hauled it back behind her head as if she hated it, into great thick stumpy plaits which were fastened with an elaborate system of hairbands, grips and slides as though against escape. The braids, joined at the ends in one even thicker stumpier plait, crouched on the back of her neck like a sullen, lumpy-looking fungus.

He toiled along under the critical eyes of yet more long-dead Noones, catching tantalising glimpses of rooms through half-open doors and fleeting views through windows. He would never ever be able to find his way around Owlcote by himself. It was worse than his first day at secondary school.

At last Harriet led him down yet more steps into an enormous room with great arching windows and there promptly abandoned him, retreating to a tapestry-covered chair and flinging herself moodily into it.

'Well, here he is,' she said aggressively to no one in particular, and then apparently tuning out, she began studying the fingers of her gloves with a fixed scowl.

5

The Cage of Shadows

The room was filled with dusk and birdsong. Peering around him, bewildered, Gerard had some initial difficulty in sorting out the shapes that were furniture from those that might turn out to be members of his own long-lost family.

There was a fire burning low with a sweet resinous smell. In front of it was a short-legged oak table set with tea things: delicate floral china and silverware, napkins of snowy linen.

The birdsong came from the window wall itself, which turned out to be one enormous aviary, from floor to ceiling. There in the blue dusk, dozens of small imprisoned birds fluttered, hopped and groomed themselves in constant agitated motion. Once he had seen them he could not take his eyes off them, nor completely tear his mind from the horror he felt at their pitiful half-life.

It was the most disturbing room Gerard had ever been in, as if nothing and no one in it was quite what it seemed, and might change at any moment into something else.

What little light there was to see by leaked and filtered through the decorative ironwork, flinging a delicate tracery of patterns around the walls so that Gerard experienced the momentary but unnerving illusion that the entire room was one exquisite shadowy birdcage.

Now he could make out a very old lady dressed entirely in black and seated very upright in a highbacked chair. In the dusk the drained whiteness of her face seemed to detach itself, floating eerily towards him like a fragile paper mask.

'Come over to me properly, boy, so I can get a good look at you,' she said. Her mouth smiled but Gerard couldn't look away from her eyes, which were as empty as holes in the air. He went reluctantly to her side where she seized him by the arm with a pouncing movement, pulling him closer still, hurting him slightly with her pinching fingers. Yet as she clutched him a strange nervous tremor ran through her as if she were as afraid of him as he felt of her. It was as if she both wished to pull him to her and push him away at the same time.

She's like a witch in a book, he thought. He had never met anyone who looked remotely as if she might be a witch before and now that he had she turned out to be his own grandmother. It flashed maliciously into his mind that Harriet would make a very suitable witch's apprentice.

With a great effort of will he forced himself to stand still while the old lady hungrily scanned his face. Perhaps, at last, she found what she dreaded or longed for, because all at once she almost threw him from her so that he staggered slightly into the tea-table, making the china cups ring musically against one another. Then she disowned her own extraordinary action by saying sharply: 'Be careful, boy. I won't have my best china broken.'

Now Gerard recognised Caroline sitting on the extreme edge of a formal brocade-covered sofa, biting her lip, her eyes downcast, and Uncle Avery beside her, remote as the moon.

'He's really so remarkably like Lindsey, it takes the breath away,' said someone.

Gerard turned gratefully in the direction of the friendly voice.

'Are you my uncle William?' he asked shyly. 'I think I saw you in the photograph.'

Uncle William waved an amiable hand. 'And now you're seeing the real thing,' he said. 'Which do you prefer?'

Will was nothing whatever like Avery. He looked so much younger and more human for one thing. Or perhaps it was not so much that he looked younger as that he appeared somehow strangely unused as if not an awful lot had happened to him yet. Though presumably in his thirties, he still dressed like a student in a pair of beaten-up, much-patched denim jeans and an old navy crew-necked sweater with moth-eaten elbows. His hair was thick and dark and needed cutting: it lapped at his collar and fell slightly into his eyes. But Gerard found himself warming to Will's humorous flexible face and his easy lazy voice.

'I must introduce you to Bee,' said Will. 'Bee is the very clever, talented and persistent lady who helped us to find you.'

'Hallo,' said Gerard, locating her in the gloom. Beatrice Summers was an intense-looking young woman with masses of tawny hair. Her enormous iridescent earrings swung and tinkled like windchimes whenever she moved.

'Do let him sit down, the poor boy,' she said. 'He looks worn out. What a frightful shock, Gerard, to find yourself related to a ruined castle and a great pile of dead ancestors. Pour him some tea, Will.' She leaned her chin on her small round hand and looked at Gerard as if she was actually interested in knowing him. For the first time since saying goodbye to Norah, he felt genuinely visible to another human being. Bee saw Gerard straight away and even seemed to like whatever it was she saw. But Beatrice didn't live here, he remembered.

'More tea, Mother?' Will unfurled long legs and loped over to the tea things.

'Please don't pour any for me,' said Gerard, full of dread. 'I'm really fine.'

He would only spill it in his lap or break one of the delicate china cups and then his witch grandmother would fix him with those awful eyes that were like greedy holes in the air and turn him into one of her birds, perhaps, and there he would be, imprisoned in this strange dusky siren-singing room forever.

'It's a beautiful room,' he gabbled with desperate politeness. 'Do you let the birds out sometimes?'

Everyone seemed relieved to have something new to talk about. They all started talking at once, explaining to him that these birds were almost all from tropical rain forests and if they were released here they would certainly die from exposure or be pecked to death by native birds. His grandmother repeated several times, her mouth tight with disapproval, that no one must ever

59

take it upon themselves to even touch the cage without permission.

Gerard had known all this. It was just that he had to give some form to the nameless anxiety welling up inside him. Somehow it was less painful, less frightening to worry about small birds imprisoned behind their pretty wrought-iron doors, and whether they would ever again be allowed to be free, than it was to let himself be swept away into other darker currents of anxiety waiting to suck him down and down out of the present moment and into — into what? He didn't know. Only that if he once gave in he would be lost.

Canute-like, he sat tensely sweating in his tapestry covered armchair, defying the invisible tide to rise up through the polished floorboards and wash around his knees.

For some reason the silences in this room panicked him just as they had unnerved him earlier with his uncle, every one wildly signalling his abject failure as a desirable long-lost relation. He never minded silences with Phil or Norah. Perhaps because they had clearly been comfortable with them too. Here, whenever someone ventured a new topic of conversation, Gerard felt quite dizzy with relief, as though he'd been thrown a lifebuoy. Bee seemed to divine his feelings and threw him quite a few.

It was Bee who raised the subject of Gerard's education. They all seemed to agree on the local comprehensive to begin with. When the Easter holidays were over, Caroline would take him to look round. Harriet, he was unsurprised to learn, went to a private school for girls. He wished she went to boarding school in the Highlands of Scotland.

After a while, Gerard, his neck prickling, became conscious that the room had gradually fallen into the longest and chilliest silence so far. It took him a moment to realise that someone was in fact speaking: his witch grandmother. Apparently it was Gerard she was addressing, though she did not at any time use his name, try to meet his eyes or even make the slightest effort to pitch her thin aristocratic voice across the drowning space between them.

'The Noones are of course your rightful family now,' she was telling the furniture behind him. 'But you will swiftly learn that living at Owlcote confers not only rights but responsibilities.' Here there was a sideways flickering glance. 'The Noones have always been remarkable for their achievements. No Noone has ever brought shame upon this house.' Another awful glance from those empty eyes. 'Thomas Noone, who built Owlcote, was himself a favourite at Elizabeth's court.'

Shifting in his chair, straining to hear the thin sibilant words as they came and went tonelessly in the air, Gerard was vaguely oppressed by her monotonous recital of famous and bloody battles at which Noones had murdered or been murdered themselves (Trafalgar, Waterloo, the Crimea), and other impressive historical events in which long-deceased Noones had played their vital part. He could tell this identical speech had been made again and again. It was as if, out of long habit, but without energy, the ancient house itself spoke through the puppet body of his grandmother. History settled on the room like layers of dust and solidified into stone strata. Gerard felt he would suffocate under the weight of all that was dead and gone and could not be changed. Slumped in her chair, her eyes glazed,

Harriet seemed scarcely to be breathing; a scowling stone girl.

'A Noone's conduct is always exemplary. But if you work hard and strive to live up to the example that has been set for you, this family will have reason to be proud of you.' She had been careful not to say, he noticed, that they *would* be proud of him. She had finished, he realised, simply returning her attention coldly to her tea cup.

The speech was over. He was dismissed. Bloody hell. Gerard, at first dazed and baffled, was now thoroughly impressed. It took his breath away how she managed to get through it all without a single reference to Lindsey; his dead mother, her runaway daughter.

Apart from that it had a depressingly familiar ring. He didn't make the mistake of imagining she was genuinely inviting him to share her golden world. He had discovered long ago that some people actually needed to keep you as a permanent outsider in order to experience being insiders themselves. You might start out well enough, shine every week in spelling tests, eat your liver and remember Mother's Day, but sooner or later you made the fatal slip; lost dinner money, trekked mud unwittingly across the clean hallway and then you were done for. Back to the bottom rung.

Remembering these things, which he had learned for himself the hard way, Gerard was surprised to find himself almost smiling. He had been so little and helpless then. Since then he had had Norah. And even before Norah he had called Lark out of the darkness. For a moment he saw her, stepping into his room, flaming like a fallen star, shaking off shadows, the smell of roses. If she was leaving him now it was because, like

Norah, she thought she had taken him as far as she could and that he would now survive. He thought she might be right.

'Well,' he said, shrugging, looking his witch grandmother directly in her dreadful vindictive eye. 'If I don't make the grade, you needn't worry. You can always send me back to Deben House.'

There was a muffled sound from Bee behind him. Even Harriet looked up, briefly roused from her gloom. But he went on, without giving anyone a chance to comment, 'Would it be all right if I just wander about here until I have to start school again? Will it be okay if I explore?'

After all, he should make the most of it. He mightn't be here long and there might never be another chance to live in a castle.

'I don't see why not – so long as you don't fall into the river too often,' said Bee, apparently highly amused about something, and rather too carefully not looking at Will who was himself sternly examining his fingernails.

But his grandmother thrust herself forward in her chair with a hissing sound. For a moment Gerard thought she was actually going to spit at Beatrice. But she only gripped the arms of her chair more tightly and Gerard saw her papery white hands tremble.

'Of course you may roam around wherever the fancy takes you,' she said, though she made even this outwardly pleasant invitation sound like a curse. 'But you must keep away from the old maze. Look at me, young man, when I'm speaking. My husband put the maze out of bounds years ago. He believed it to be an unlucky place. In our family we all honour his wishes so you

63

will also be expected to. Is that clear? Providing you behave yourself, you have the freedom of the entire park except for the maze.'

He dropped his eyes. 'Yes,' he muttered. 'Yes. Thank you.'

So that was what Lark had shown him out of his attic window. A maze. He was forbidden to go there. Yet it was only the maze which called to him.

The rest of his day passed in a blur of exhaustion. But before he finally fell, numb with tiredness into his strange bed in his lonely tower room, he couldn't resist one last look out of his window.

It was too dark to see anything. The moon was behind cloud. But still he stared and stared out into the invisible garden, sensing the direction of the maze, knowing it was waiting for him, restlessly pulling him to it like the tides to the hidden moon.

He had never entered a maze. He imagined it like the drawings in comics. Trace the right path with your finger until you find the hidden treasure or the lost child.

'Earth, Water, Fire, Air,' sang the small blank voice in his head. 'Met together in a garden fair. Put in a basket bound with skin. If you answer this riddle . . .'

He was too tired. Ever since the car had crossed over the river that ran quietly through the village of soft golden stone, he had been hearing disembodied voices.

Not voices, he thought. The same voice. There was only one.

'*Terra, Aquae, Ignis, Aeris,*' said the girl, clear and sharply conversational in the darkness of his room. 'That's Latin. In his books it is written in Latin.'

Gerard wheeled around, his scalp prickling. This was

beyond any daydream, any self-deception. He didn't know Latin. He couldn't imagine Latin. Yet someone had spoken Latin to him, he knew it.

'Who are you? Come out so I can see you.'

There was no one there of course.

I'm overtired. I'm just overtired.

He crawled into his bed, pulling the covers up around his ears. Just before he slept he thought, oh I do hope Errol's all right without me.

And then, unknowing, he dropped down through darkness to where the maze was waiting and at its heart a girl in a dirty white shift, her hair falling in her face, in her hand a small dark unstoppered bottle.

6

Harriet No one

Gerard slept late and only managed a brief exploration of part of the west wing of the house before he set off to meet Harriet.

Owlcote, he thought, had a disconnected feel, as if each room existed by itself in lonely isolation rather than as part of a living whole. The room that struck Gerard as the friendliest, next to the kitchen, was the little sitting room, where the twins watched children's television and Caroline caught up with the papers or did a bit of sewing.

The dining room was too grand and stiff for Gerard. He guessed it was the room the family used when Avery brought important clients home.

Many of the rooms were badly in need of repair. Trying a door that stuck fast Gerard wondered if Avery kept the old house going because he really loved it, despite his complaints, or if he ever sneakily longed for an ordinary three-bedroomed semi. Perhaps he felt responsible to all those stern, long-faced, dead and gone Noones, or even to Thomas Noone and his larger than life dreams. Perhaps the dining room was to impress them, not Avery's clients after all. He tapped his knuckles against a stretch of oak panelling and it sounded satisfyingly hollow, summoning up fantasies of secret rooms or passages.

But the next door was the prize, opening gloriously into a vast galleried central hall with the most elaborate ceiling he had ever seen; all carved wooden Tudor roses and fleurs-de-lys and laughing mythical beasts that twined themselves around massive pillars like fantastic vines.

There were more portraits in the gallery. Gerard thought one of them was of the Elizabethan alchemist himself. He was not actually a physically large man and he was obviously trying his best to wear the pursed, vinegary, looking-down-the-nose expression that Elizabethans wore when they had their portraits painted, but he couldn't keep the reckless laughter completely out of his eyes.

There was something impressive about him, thought Gerard. It was not just that he appeared to glow with health and vigour. It was his breathtaking confidence in himself and his place in the world. It made him think of the kind of man who suddenly sells up his house to sail around the world single-handed.

Across more than four centuries the first master of Owlcote stared out as though across unmapped oceans; his adventurer's eyes burning a steady furious undiminished blue.

You'd be a wonderful friend when everything was going well, thought Gerard, tearing his own eyes away almost reluctantly. But I wouldn't like to be around you when things got tough.

Gerard's trainers left prints in the dust and when he touched one of the walls the plaster was wet, crumbling under his hand with a dank smell of mushrooms.

Beneath the window a clump of fiddlehead fern unfurled, where it had pushed its way vigorously through from outside. Gerard shivered, understanding now why the Elizabethans weren't so keen on Nature in the wild. It did make you feel rather small and temporary somehow.

Once this hall was filled with light and warmth and the sound of voices, perhaps laughter and music and dancing feet. Standing in the middle of the ruins of the Elizabethan hall, Gerard felt unnervingly close to those ghostly revellers.

It was a happy house in the beginning.

'What happened?' he said automatically.

Then he realised with a flash of fear, remembering the disembodied voice in his room, that he could no longer be sure it was Lark who had spoken to him. Everything was mixed up here. Perhaps it was possible to be multiply haunted. He supposed it must be. Or just singly mad, he thought glumly.

Carefully, feeling slightly frayed at either possibility, he closed the great oak door on the neglected hall and set off for his appointment with his cousin. He had quite enough to deal with in the material world, he thought.

Harriet was late, having arrived by the most devious and confusing route possible in order, she explained in her hostile voice, to avoid detection.

'Isn't it a shame the maze is banned,' said Gerard. 'That would have been a good place to meet.'

'You must be joking,' said Harriet with scorn. 'I went in there just as soon as I could after I was old enough to realise it was off limits. There's absolutely nothing to it but hedge and gravel, gravel and hedge. Boring, boring, boring.' She laughed as Gerard's face fell. 'You should just see your expression.'

Harriet looked fiercer and wilder than ever this morning. Gerard unkindly thought she rather resembled a bolting horse, checked in its flight and forced to a shuddering standstill.

Today she had hauled her hair back from her face into plaits so tautly that her forehead fairly bulged with the stress of it. She was dressed in severe navy with a touch of white where her shirt collar showed above her sweater. Though it was not cold, she wore gloves. Not a schoolgirl's gloves today but black lacy evening gloves with scalloped edges and tiny ornamental jet beads. The effect of this distinctly mixed message was startling, as if she'd appeared in a scarlet evening dress with flippers.

For a while his cousin strode back and forth in frozen silence, her head lowered between her round shoulders, scowling down at her beetle-crusher shoes and Gerard, now wishing very much that he had simply failed to turn up, began to think of excuses so he could have the rest of the morning to himself.

Then abruptly she stopped pacing at the point where two rather battered ornamental lions guarded a shallow flight of steps and perched herself on the topmost step, glaring up at him under thick dark brows with eyes that even through her spectacles were visibly opaque with misery.

'I know just what you're thinking,' she ground out. 'You're thinking, "She's rather out of context in this place," aren't you? Be honest.'

Saying this seemed to cost her a great deal. In fact Gerard had thought nothing of the kind after his initial mild surprise.

'I think I had expected you'd be blonde and a bit

69

horsey,' he admitted, grinning at the contrast between his fantasy cousin and this all-too-real one.

'So you were surprised,' she pushed.

'Harriet – this is all one big surprise to me. A few weeks ago I was just this boy in a kid's home, with no one of my own. But I knew how I felt about myself and who I was and all that stuff. Or I thought I did. Now – well, I'm in one great muddle now. You can't begin to imagine.'

'I'm adopted, you see,' Harriet continued, pursuing her own gloomy theme with the morbid determination of someone deaf to everything but the quarrel going on inside her own head. 'That's how I came to be a Noone. They couldn't have kids of their own. So they were told anyway. So they decided to do the world a good turn and adopt me. Hard to Place, they called black kids up for adoption then. Social worker jargon for out of context. They called me Harriet after *her* because she was so furious about the whole thing. For some pathetic reason they thought it might win her round. Rather like trying to wheedle your way round the bloody Sphinx if you ask me. Anyway, four years ago my parents had sweet little fair-haired twins of their very own. The doctors had been wrong all the time. So Avery and Caroline needn't have put themselves through all the bother. But of course it was a bit late by then. Rather bad luck for them, don't you think?'

Listening to his cousin, Gerard felt as if someone were forcing him to walk very slowly and deliberately across a sea of broken glass. Harriet was one of the most uncomfortable people he had ever been with. Not knowing what to say for the best, he stayed tactfully quiet. He guessed she wouldn't hear much anyone else said to her anyway.

What Harriet seemed to need most of all was a listener and Gerard had been a skilful listener for most of his life. At weak moments, even foster mothers had poured out their woes to him. But from this he had learned the hard way that, far from feeling closer to you, people sometimes hated you afterwards for knowing the secrets they themselves had willingly spilled out. Gerard wished Norah was here. She would know what to say and what not to say. But Harriet was still talking relentlessly.

'There's things someone should tell you about this family.' She swung her foot moodily over the side of the steps. Her sock slid down a fraction, exposing a dry ashy-looking knee. At once she strained it back into position. 'You've already heard all the PR.'

'PR?' Gerard sat cautiously astride the grizzled head of the second heraldic lion.

'Public Relations. Granny Noone's obnoxious spiel about the Noble Noones and how you must be sure to strive night and day nor let your sword sleep in your hand and all that, to live up to their ghastly example. I bet Dad gave you the same garbage? Yes, don't be so bloody polite. I knew he would. There ought to be a word that means the opposite of public relations, didn't there? The underside. The part people hide from other people and never talk about and refuse to admit is there even to themselves. You won't want to believe it either you know, cousin Gerard. I warn you.'

She put up a gloved hand and, groping blindly, checked and then checked again her complex arrangement of elastic bands. She twisted one of them round an extra couple of times.

'Honestly, Gerard, I don't think I can stand it if you don't believe me. I know I'm completely mad to confide in you. I've absolutely no reason to trust you. But you're my last chance, you see,' she finished up, still not looking at him.

'If you don't get on with it and tell me, you'll never know, will you?' said Gerard, whose patience was wearing thin.

'I know,' she said, still studying her knees. 'But until I've actually told you, I can hang on to the thought that you might believe me, you see. Like keeping a sweet under your pillow when you're little, for when they switch out the light and leave you alone.'

'I don't make a habit of going around disbelieving people, Harriet. Just to spite them. Why shouldn't I believe you? You don't look like a liar to me. Honestly, I'm well up on liars and you haven't got the look.'

She stared at him with her opaque, molasses-coloured eyes, her face bleak, shut. She gave a deep apprehensive sigh. Under her eyes, behind the glint of her glasses, were fine spiderwebs of shadow as if she didn't sleep much. She got to her feet and swallowed so hard that Gerard found himself swallowing in sympathy.

'I want you to help me stop the family curse,' she blurted out.

She was already backing away, ready to bolt, her shoulders hunched, her brows glowering. 'Go on – laugh at me,' she said in her hostile jeering voice. 'You want to, don't you? You're thinking, "She's got bats in her belfry, but I'll keep on looking deadly polite and humour her." They all do that. Bee – even Bee . . .'

'If you just calmed down for a minute and looked at me, really looked at me as if I was a real person,' said

Gerard, 'you'd see that I don't even want to laugh or grin or even smirk a tiny bit. Don't tell me what I feel. It makes me feel – quite – I don't know – invisible. For Heaven's sake just tell me what you mean. You really mean an actual curse? A real deadly curse that strikes down all the Noones in the summer of their days, or just the eldest sons or what?'

'It doesn't exactly strike them down,' said Harriet warily. 'But it is deadly and it's real all right. It's the realest thing in the whole rotten house. I don't know when it started or who began it. As far as I can see it's been here forever. But the terrible thing is that it's as if no one else but me can see it. I used to think it was because I was a sort of outsider. Only a Noone by adoption. Or because I'm still quite young. And because they're older they've all got used to it – the way you get used to the taste of the water in your own home so it doesn't actually seem to have a taste at all, if you see what I mean. Well, you're a sort of outsider, Gerard, and you're the same age as me. So I thought perhaps you'd be able to see it too.'

She had taken something out of her skirt pocket and, stooping down, was doing something on the steps with small scratching sounds that set his teeth on edge. When she had finished, she stood back and let him see what she had done.

'If you write it like that, with a space between the O's,' she said, with an odd smile, 'it doesn't look quite so grand and ancestral, does it?'

Gerard felt his scalp prickle.

NO ONE, she had scribbled again and again. NO ONE NO ONE NO ONE.

'Why did you do that?' he asked, repelled. 'Whatever

73

was the point of doing that?' Something in him was shaken. He felt a surge of anger towards her. But she was still regarding him with her odd bitter smile.

'It's what the curse does, that's the point,' she said. 'Why do you think they all make such a song and dance about the Noble Noone bit? I'll tell you. It's because deep inside they know that in the end the Noones always get rubbed out little by little by little – a little more each day without them noticing it – from the inside out until there's nothing left at all except the noble *shell*. Oh they start out like everyone else. Full of dreams and plans – my grandfather, my dad, my uncle Will – and they end up – No one.'

She took off her glasses and scrubbed angrily at her face before she replaced them.

'It's just as if at some point, just as their lives are going swimmingly, it all goes wrong. As if one day they wake up to find written on their bedroom mirror in fiery letters: YOU'LL NEVER HAVE YOUR HEART'S DESIRE. And then they just give up. All the fight goes out of them. And even if they almost get their dream, at the last moment it twists and turns upon them like a knife in the air.

'Look at Uncle Will. He had a book of poems published when he was still very young, early twenties. Everyone said he was the most talented young poet since – oh I don't know – Yeats or Keats or something. He was all set to be this genius poet. Went off to London like Dick Whittington. Then suddenly back he came to Owlcote to live with Granny Noone again and start up his stupid organic apple juice business in the stables. And he hasn't written another word except letters to the *Guardian* about "the imminent destruction

74

of the ecosystem". He just ambles about like a big kid and makes out everything is one big joke — because what's the point of *anything* when we're all going to be blown up anyway. He tells everyone he's working on a great unfinished epic poem about nuclear winter but I bet he hasn't written anything for over a year. I don't know why Bee doesn't ditch him. I know she will in the end. And well — I used to think — '

Her glasses came off again and her voice wavered, almost failing her. 'Well, it won't get me. I needn't care. Because I'm not a Noone. My real father was a student, Gerard. He was going to be an archaeologist. I'm his as much as theirs. When I was little I used to dream about finding him, going along to help him, you know, dig up the ancient African cities of gold and stuff. Pathetic, wasn't it.'

She glared into space for a while. 'But then I realised it was starting to work on me. The curse. Like all the rest of them. And that's why you've got to help me. Because I *won't* be like them. I'd rather die than end up like them — '

Gerard was feeling very uncomfortable. He both did and didn't want to believe her. It was obvious that Harriet was desperately sincere but in itself that wasn't much help. Perhaps, he thought, what Harriet was describing so melodramatically was only actually something depressingly ordinary. The sort of thwarted dreams and vanished hopes any family might have. Misery was misery. Why dignify it by assuming there was something occult about it?

Gerard could make secret space in his universe for unofficial manifestations like Lark. He could even believe in the reality of long-lost families that surfaced after twelve years like a city believed drowned under the sea.

But family curses? That belonged to the realm of croaking ravens and . . . ruined castles, he thought, with an alarmed sense of being trapped by his own deductive processes.

And what about a voice that spoke Latin to you in the middle of the night?

He wondered if Harriet learned Latin at her posh school.

'It was after the twins were born,' she went on, seating herself again on the scarred head of the companion stone lion. 'And even that, you see – having them was Dad's heart's desire. I'd never seen him like that before. So proud, like those tribes where the men have the labour pains and all the glory and the women slip off and get it over with under a tree. But Caroline was really ill having them and they were born too early and since then they've both been in and out of hospital all their lives. They're allergic to just about everything. Sometimes I think Mum and Dad should just shut them up inside a gigantic glass bubble where they can't be contaminated by the ordinary world. Mum sort of tries to do that anyway, fussing over them all the time, monitoring every change of expression. She'd breathe for them if she could. Dad can't stand it sometimes. They don't fight exactly, but – '

'You were telling me how you knew the curse had started on you,' said Gerard, feeling tired and on edge. It was obvious Harriet hadn't talked to anyone for a long time but he felt unpleasantly as if she was unpicking the seams of his new life before his eyes, like a piece of bad knitting, forcing him to look at all the snarls and

76

flaws before he'd had a chance to form opinions of his own.

'I'm *trying* to. Don't you think I know I look like the biggest idiot in the world babbling on like this. I'm trying to show you how it gets hold of your most – most precious thing, your dearest dream or wish and turns it into – into *ashes*. Listen – believe it or not, Gerard, I've always been quite clever. I could read ages before I went to school. No one really taught me. I just learned. I always picked up everything really fast and even though some of the teachers obviously thought poor old Avery and Caroline had really landed themselves with some kind of factory second, I soon showed them. I won prizes for everything, even without meaning to, or even trying very hard. And each time I started something new and found it easy, Mum was really dopey and excited about it. Like – This is it! This is Harriet's thing. We can all relax. She's going to turn out all right.

'And then I started to learn the piano and I picked that up quickly too. But I loved it. Oh, Gerard, I loved it.' She looked down, clenching her gloved hands tightly in her lap. 'Then one day I heard Daddy talking to Granny Noone and they didn't know I was there. And she said: "Oh, Avery, darling, by now it's tediously obvious to all of us that everything that sour little witch touches will turn to gold. And what good will it do her in the end. She'll end up just like the rest of us." And then I knew – I knew. It was going to get its claws into me too. Like an owl. I think of it like an owl in a nightmare I used to have, sort of horribly sucking all the light into itself. The Owlcote owl. Laurie sometimes dreams about it now.'

'I don't understand,' said Gerard, increasingly uneasy. 'How did you know?' Something was troubling him but he couldn't bring it up to the surface of his mind. It bobbed around out of reach and sank whenever he got near, like something drowning. It was what she said about gold.

GOLD, CURSE – Lark had written with the Scrabble tiles.

While Harriet was speaking he kept getting renewed depthcharges of the carsick feeling he had experienced as they drove over the bridge, only this time it seemed to spread rippling outwards from his own person so that the river and the trees and the fabric of the park itself, quivered as though with heat haze.

'Don't you know the story?' Harriet was demanding. 'About the king and everything he touched – '

'Yes of course I do. Even my education isn't that defective. It was in my reading book or something when I was seven. But why are you hanging so much on one stupid catty remark? I bet she was just feeling really jealous and grudging about how well you'd turned out after she'd objected to them adopting you.'

'It wasn't only that,' said Harriet barely audibly. She had talked herself out. She looked ill. 'But there's no use telling you any more.'

Suddenly she sprang up, backing away from him. 'I wish I'd never told you!' she shouted. 'I knew you wouldn't understand anything and I was right. Listen you stupid, stupid boy. Everything that Midas loved died when he touched it. Gold should have been a blessing but instead it was just another way of killing. If I'd been adopted by another family I could be anything – anything I dreamed of. But not now. Not

78

here. Here all the gifts turn into curses. Whatever I touch will die too. The life will just bleed out of it. I stopped playing, Gerard. I couldn't do it. The music was dying under my hand. It was turning meaningless like white sound. The only safe thing is not to care about anything. Anything at all.'

She was staring at Gerard who was appalled and speechless. Her eyes were like her grandmother's: bleak holes in the air. She held out her long thin hands to him in their bizarre covering of black lace.

'Why do you think I wear these!' she cried, shrill, ugly as a gull. Then she turned and loped away, awkward, round-shouldered, her head down like some brooding wounded beast.

I'd rather die than end up like them.

Was that how Lindsey felt?

Gerard had hoped to get closer to his mother here, in her own home, but she had receded even further. With every hour he spent at Owlcote she became lonelier, more elusive, more enigmatic. Was that the curse too?

I'd rather die —

Was that why she let herself be killed by a speeding car on a dark street? Had she run so far from her family and Owlcote to escape the curse's clutches, only to find she carried its darkness within her like a deadly virus all the time?

I think of it like an owl. The Owlcote owl.

Unhappy and alone, he longed for someone who could give him answers. He longed most of all for Lark the way she was before. But no one came.

7

A Shoe Box

For the next half hour or so, Gerard wandered aimlessly around the grounds, all his pleasure in exploration gone, yet reluctant to go back into the house and risk running into his cousin. He felt wretched; every inch a displaced person. It had all gone wrong so quickly. Well, he thought, it had never really been right.

It was with a feeling of relief that he finally ran into his uncle Will who had just parked his van by the stables and also seemed down in the dumps.

'Just taken Bee to the station,' he said. 'Her car's in dock. She had to get back to London.'

'I would have said goodbye,' said Gerard. 'I didn't know – it was really nice of her to try to find me for you and everything.' He fell into step as well as he could.

Will looked a bit confused. 'Beatrice is a rather remarkable girl,' he admitted. But he said it in such a way that Gerard suspected some of the remarkable qualities included ones disruptive to Will's own easy-going existence.

'Do you want to take a look around the stables?' Will suggested. 'Can you spare a minute or two? I'll make you a cup of coffee if you like.'

Grateful for both distraction and company, Gerard followed his uncle around the converted outbuildings, admiring the old apple press and the great barrels stacked everywhere.

'Spanish oak,' Will told him. 'Hundreds of years old, some of them. For some reason nothing else does the job so well. This is the bottling machine and over here's some of the actual stuff we produce.'

He indicated shelves of bottles full of golden liquid, each of them labelled 'Owlcote Original Organic Apple Juice' with a rustic-looking label.

'There's nothing much doing here this time of year of course. But it hots up like anything in the summer. People bring apples by the lorryload. I have to get help from the village.'

'Is it nice working here? Do you like doing this?' asked Gerard, Harriet's words about the curse of the Noones still ringing in his ears.

Will thought for a while before he answered and then he said with a rather sad smile, 'There are two kinds of actions in the world, you know, Gerard. The kind that hurt people and the kind that don't. I just do my best not to hurt people and this seems about as harmless as anything you could find, wouldn't you agree?'

Gerard nodded uncertainly, not so much because he agreed but because he was sure that Will was a kind person who didn't want to harm anyone. Privately he thought Will's division of human acts into two kinds a bit oversimplified. He didn't like the idea of hurting people himself. But unless you lived your life as some kind of boneless jelly person, surely, it sometimes couldn't be helped?

'Bee doesn't agree with me,' said Will unexpectedly. 'She says I should join that religious cult in India or wherever it is, the people who wear masks whenever

81

they go out so as not to kill a single insect by accidentally inhaling it.'

This made Gerard want to laugh. He could just imagine Bee saying that in her forthright voice.

'Her father's a vet,' said Will rather glumly, as though her callousness might be inherited. 'The stairs are out here.'

He led the way up rickety ladder-like steps on the outside of the stables and let them both into his small untidy apartment, which he called 'The Apple Loft'. The loft did smell very strongly of fermenting apples, as if, over the years, the golden juice had soaked into the walls and joists and floors, becoming part of them. Gerard liked it but it made him feel slightly light-headed.

'Milk? Sugar?' asked Will, plugging in an ancient kettle and piling heaps of coffee-stained papers on top of other heaps.

Gerard wondered if any of these contained parts of Will's unfinished poem. There was an uncovered typewriter with a sheet of paper in it. He could just make out the words, 'Dear Editor'.

'Both please,' he said, realising too late that he was snooping.

'It's okay,' said Will, seeing him jump. 'Please feel free to look around.'

'I thought at first it was stained glass,' said Gerard, looking with pleasure at the windows. They were covered with bright translucent stickers of leaping dolphins, rainbows, peace symbols and mythical trees whose roots transformed themselves with a creative swirl into the planet Earth and whose leaves were crowded with glowing fruit and radiant doves.

Gerard felt at home at once. It reminded him of the cottage Phil shared with his young wife Jess and their new baby when he was not at Deben House. Phil was a Friend of the Earth too. He was always trying, without success, to interest the older kids in weeding the rambling overgrown garden and starting a compost heap.

Without waiting to be asked, Gerard found himself a corner of a sagging couch near the brightly coloured window, so that he was squashed between a pile of paperbacks on famine and acid rain on one side and a rather predatory scented geranium on the other. The window sill, he noticed, was overflowing with exuberant greenery.

Wincing, Gerard prised a crumpled pamphlet out from under himself. It was titled, *Antarctica, the Last Wilderness*. A large number of the other books on Will's shelves seemed to be on similarly depressing subjects and on the wall were posters lamenting vanishing rain forests and various endangered species.

Gerard felt exhausted at this unflinching inventory of Paradises lost, poisoned and plundered by man's greed and stupidity. It would drive him mad, he thought, to have to look at the world destroying itself each time he looked up. He could only bear it in small doses.

He thought of Norah who would only let herself watch the news once a week. Her life, she said, was only just long enough to deal with what was immediately in front of her. 'My name's not Atlas. I can't take on the grief of the world. And agonizing about it without doing a damn thing to change it isn't any use to anybody.'

Gerard and Will drank their Traidcraft coffee and

talked about nothing very much, yet in an easy companionable way, which Gerard found something of a relief after his morning with Harriet. But after a while, looking up from a book Will was showing him about American Indian tribes in which, it turned out, they were both interested, he caught his uncle watching him with a gentle, sad expression as though he were gazing through Gerard to someone else.

'You are so like her,' he said apologetically. 'It's quite unnerving, you know. The way you move your hands. The way you hold your head. Your eyes – you're absolutely the living image of her.'

'I didn't know,' said Gerard, looking down confused, feeling himself flush with astonished pleasure. 'I've only got one picture of her and she looks so anonymous. She could be anyone's mother.'

'I've only got one that I know of,' said Will. 'But you're welcome to it if I can find it. I'll dig it out for you if I can.' He began rummaging through cupboards and drawers in what looked to be a hopeless task.

'You don't mind talking about her?' asked Gerard, hardly daring to hope. 'It doesn't upset you or anything? Only no one else seems to want to mention her, as if they've convinced themselves I got here from out of a test-tube or something.'

'Lindsey was practically the best thing that ever happened in this family,' said Will, his head inside a bureau. 'There was never anyone like her. Oh, she seemed such a quiet mousy child to begin with, a dreamy little girl, loving and pliant, so willing to please everyone and fit in with us all just so long as people loved her in return. But as she grew up, she became more and more private, she seemed to make up her

84

mind there was something she wanted that she could never find here at Owlcote – and once Lindsey really made her mind up, you couldn't budge her.'

He transferred the search to a large cabin trunk, dumping great piles of papers on the floor beside him before he went on. Gerard's heart skipped a beat. Will was talking about Lindsey as if he had genuinely loved her and missed having her around. It made him feel as if, invisibly, she had entered the room. Although it was something he deeply desired, it almost frightened him, this powerful new awareness of her.

To displace his anxiety he began to study the titles of some crumbling old leather-bound volumes stacked under a chair. *Paracelsus*, he read. *The Way of Alchemy. The Twelve Keys. The Alchemist's Quest.*

'Once,' said Will, 'she really took exception to something they tried to make her do at school. She just refused. The teacher said she had to do it and she said, no, she wouldn't and they couldn't make her. Then she walked calmly out of the door and walked home three miles over the fields to Owlcote. She never went back. She said she wouldn't go back to that school no matter what they did to her. And she didn't. Though my mother and father did everything they could to make her. Well, Mother did and Father went along with it for a quiet life the way he usually did. He was something of an absent father, if you know what I mean, Gerry. I mean he was there physically, but not *really* there, if you can understand me. He was pleasant enough if he was absolutely forced to stay in the same room with you, but somehow you could never really reach him.'

Gerard nodded, thinking of Avery.

'In the end they sent her away to a ghastly Dickensian

85

kind of boarding school, to curb her spirit, Mother said. But I don't think it did. I think it just made it easier for her to break away from us all in the end.'

Will sat back on his heels and shook his hair out of his eyes. Now he was closer to him, Gerard could see that his uncle's tousled dark curls were faintly threaded with silver.

'Here,' said Will. 'I've found it.' He handed a little square of paper over to Gerard, letting another flutter to the floor as he did so.

'Oh,' said Gerard, saddened. 'Thank you – but it's the same as my one.'

'Oh bad luck,' said Will, equally downcast. 'It doesn't look much like her, as a matter of fact. Looks sort of fugitive, doesn't she? Yet quite honestly, in her quiet way Lindsey was the strongest of us all. Once, just before she left, she said that she had learnt a long time ago, that if you weren't given what you needed to survive, sometimes you simply had to take it and I think that's why she went. She at least had the courage to love someone with all her heart and go after what she needed no matter what – what anyone else said,' he finished up uncertainly, as if his mind had strayed, and began putting everything back into the trunk. Gerard understood that Will didn't know how to begin to talk to him about the man Lindsey had fallen in love with, run away with: Gerard's father. Another absent father.

'Let me help,' said Gerard. 'You dropped this one, look. Who's the little boy with the boat?'

Laughing out at him from a fading holiday snap, was an endearing small child clutching a toy yacht, the sun in his eyes.

'Can't you recognise him? I suppose he has changed quite a bit. It's Avery, when he was about four.'

'Are you sure?'

'Perfectly. Look. Here's another later one.'

But Gerard was still staring open-mouthed. He would have known the child in the second photograph without being told: a bony, supercillious boy of perhaps seven years old, hair shorn high above his ears, frozen smile hovering above his too-tight collar and tie, evasive eyes. But the first child — whatever could have happened to turn this glowing, vulnerable child, brimming with life and mischief, into the impermeably sealed man his uncle Avery had become? How could that happen to a person just between the taking of one family photograph and another?

It was a happy house in the beginning.

Will closed the lid of the box, sighing. He seemed troubled again, uneasy suddenly. 'I hope you won't think me unfriendly, Gerard,' he said abruptly, 'but I've got a bit of work to catch up on. Come round another time, won't you. I'm really sorry about the photo.' Then chewing his underlip for a moment he glanced away from Gerard before he said, too casually, 'But if you'd like to have them I've got these little bits and pieces she left behind, just children's things, you know. Jottings. Drawings. She used to sit up in that tower room of yours for hours on her own, playing make-believe.'

'It was her room?' said Gerard. It was like being given an unexpected present. They had not just been fobbing him off with some second-best attic, deliberately remote from the rest of the family. It had been Will's idea, he remembered. Will had thought Gerard would feel closer to his mother there.

87

'Not strictly her room,' said Will. 'But as I told you, Lindsey had a quiet way of taking what she needed and in the end it became hers.'

He held out a battered shoe box. 'I never really knew why I was keeping this but now I'm glad that I did. It's nothing exciting, you know. She was such a funny little girl, always daydreaming about the people that used to live at Owlcote, making up stories about them. Sometimes I think they were more real to her than we were. But perhaps you can make something of it. Once I thought I could, you see, put something together out of it all. Wrestle some kind of truth out of it. Find a pattern. There's probably some stuff of mine in there too by the way, but I don't need it. I won't be able to do anything with it now. You can just heave it out, unless you can find a use for it. Paper aeroplanes or something. Funny – each generation thinks it will change things, doesn't it? But it all goes on just the same.'

He smiled, a painful sort of smile.

'Yes,' said Gerard, not sure if he should smile back. 'Okay. Thank you very much.'

But Will wasn't actually looking at him properly any more, his gentle amiable face suddenly too carefully, almost coldly composed, so that Gerard saw all at once a startling and most unwelcome resemblance to Uncle Avery.

Lindsey was the best thing that ever happened to the family, Will had said, as if her loss had blighted fragile longings of his own.

Then for some reason Gerard found himself remembering the Gift, and his secret belief that the bone bobbin was some kind of crazy, if so far indecipherable, time-lapse message from his mother. And now he was convinced that his uncle, too, had given him another coded message. And although Will had tried to make it seem all very casual; mentioning the room, just happening to give him this old shoe box full of the past, he had not finally been able to conceal, even by turning away, the awakening of some wild hope. So that, seeing it, Gerard too experienced a pang and for a long while afterwards felt a resonating sadness.

Yet clambering down the rickety stairs, Gerard realised that Will had given him a picture of his mother that was far more precious than some squinting, out-of-focus person on a beach on some long-forgotten holiday. Lindsey had acquired her elusive third dimension at last. And Gerard was her living image. He shared her eyes, her gestures. He even shared the room she had taken for her own, and filled with her dreams, her loneliness. But Lindsey was never content to be a victim. She found the strength to go looking for the love she never had. Perhaps the Owlcote curse got its hooks into her in the end, but she hadn't surrendered without a fight.

Am I really like her? he wondered.

It seemed to him that he was and that it showed, for both Harriet and Will had somehow recognised it, and this was why they had asked him to help them, each in their own way.

On his last night at Deben House, Norah had told him his new family needed him as much as he needed them. At the time he had hardly listened. It was a figure of speech, the kind of thing people said. But now he believed Norah understood more than she knew. You've got to help me, it's my last chance, Harriet had said. Now he thought he knew what she meant. She'd blurted it out all wrong, but she'd picked him to help her in the first place because he was Lindsey's son – and because he wasn't a victim either.

Making his way across the grass in sunlight Gerard discovered to his surprise that it was now possible to go back into the house and face Harriet across the lunch table. Not just possible. Necessary.

8

Paradise Lost

But Harriet was not at lunch, she'd taken herself off in a huff to some private haunt. So as Uncle Avery was lunching in Stamford, this just left Gerard and his aunt to eat what she deprecatingly called her 'stew', a molten concoction of lamb and apricots which Gerard thought must be one of the best things he had ever tasted in his life.

The twins picked dutifully at their sombre rations, though Caroline had added sprigs of watercress, slices of tomato and so on, in an attempt to cheer things up.

From time to time Flora forgot her food completely, and simply sat staring at Gerard out of her enormous, pale, watery blue eyes, dreamily sucking the tip of her spoon; until her mother noticed and reminded her to eat.

Gerard enjoyed sitting at the large pine table, just the four of them. Harriet must be mad to miss a meal like this. Caroline was right, he thought, about her kitchen. It was an oasis of light and warmth and she was its centre. He could tell that it was important to her to be the sort of mother that was always there, dispensing sympathy and home baking, as if, perhaps, she hadn't always had them herself.

He was on the verge of confiding that he had thought he might do some kind of catering course when he left school. It was hard to think what could be better than spending your life making nice things to eat. It appealed to every part of him. The closest you could get in real life, he thought, to that soft-focus cream of leek dream of homecoming. But when it came to it, he found that this vague blueprint for some dimly perceived future was not yet ready to be brought out and exposed to the light, even to someone as apparently gentle and sympathetic as his aunt. So instead, his eye caught by the dazzle of light on Caroline's gold wedding ring, as she cleared dishes from the table, Gerard suddenly remembered the dusty old volumes stacked under Will's chair, and asked, 'Do you know much about alchemy? I thought it was just something in books. I hadn't ever heard anyone *talk* about it until the other day and now it seems to keep cropping up all the time.'

'Avery's been telling you some family history,' said his aunt. 'But perhaps he didn't tell you why Thomas Noone got obsessed with alchemy?'

'No,' said Gerard, rather startled by the change in his aunt's tone. 'Can you tell me or is it a dark secret or something?'

Caroline looked at him oddly. 'It's not a secret,' she said. 'But you're right – I do find it rather disturbing to talk about. I can't really properly explain why. Sometimes, I know it's silly, I almost convince myself that it's become part of the house just as much as the stone and timbers. And if you live here for any time, the story somehow seems to seep into your cells or your bloodstream and become part of you too. To begin with this house must have been such a happy house . . .' she was withdrawing from him into her own thoughts, as though into some private darkness, tracing a pattern in spilled salt on the wooden table.

It was a happy house in the beginning, thought Gerard.

'And of course it still is a happy house, of course it is, though all families have their ups and downs, good gracious – ' Caroline amended hastily, scooping up the salt into her palm and disposing of it. 'But I often think what a happy man Thomas Noone was in the early days of his marriage. When he built this house. Full of exuberant dreams for the future. I think their early days here were almost perfect. They wanted to share their happiness with everyone. After they moved in, they held a great midsummer party with musicians on the lawn and dancing, and alms distributed to the poor at the gate. The works. All in honour of his wife's birthday. Thomas was devoted to his wife, Katherine, you know. Her portrait is on the staircase if you're interested. She wasn't a beauty by anyone's standards, but she was all the world to him and more.'

'What happened?'

'She died. They all died. All except Thomas Noone. She was buried with the latest baby in her arms. It was the plague. Thomas Noone believed he had brought it back from London in a parcel of silks for his wife and daughters. He never forgave himself, they say, and after her death he never slept or shed a tear, only paced and paced, dry-eyed and silent. Then he started behaving oddly. Locking himself away in a room at the far end of the house and forbidding anyone the key. Staying away for weeks on end and neglecting his house and estates and coming back exhausted and feverish, only to be off again at sunrise the next day. Even when he was at home he wouldn't see his old friends and neighbours. The only person he would allow the servants to admit, was a rather disreputable character who had once been an Oxford scholar, Cornelius Ashmole.'

'And he was an alchemist, was he?' asked Gerard.

'So slander has it. Hoping to siphon off as much of Thomas Noone's fortune as he could, having rapidly run through his own. Alchemy was a pretty expensive hobby, demanding a steady supply of rare ingredients and in order to obtain them it was sometimes necessary to travel to out of the way places and perhaps behave in not entirely honest ways. It wasn't unknown for alchemists to trick or steal from each other. Yet there were other alchemists who shared their secrets, even writing books about their work, but written in such strange and difficult language to safeguard their mysteries that it was like a code that could only be cracked by the persistent seeker, the genuine man of wisdom.'

'I don't think perhaps I really understand what alchemy was,' said Gerard. 'Wasn't it just trying to turn rubbishy metals into gold?'

'For some alchemists it was,' agreed Caroline. 'And maybe that was the kind Cornelius Ashmole was. But I don't believe it was gold as such that Thomas Noone was searching for. You see there was always another side to alchemy. You should talk to Will about it really. He knows much more than I do. He got really keen on the subject a few years ago.'

'No, please, go on. I'd like you to tell me about the other side,' persisted Gerard, sure that Caroline was getting close to something important. GOLD, Lark had written, CURSE. Harriet talked about turning things to gold, and gifts to curses. The great house of the Noone family had emerged from the extraordinary energies of an Elizabethan alchemist and survived into the nineteen eighties. Had Thomas Noone's dreams also survived his death, the way Caroline said, like a ghostly house within a house?

'Well, it might sound rather silly to modern people,' she said uncomfortably, 'but although alchemy did become a sort of eccentric foster parent to chemistry in the end, I think alchemists operated more like poets or magicians than the scientists we have today. And for them gold was this symbol of all that was most perfect in the universe. Some alchemists believed that, through their work, they were entering into really sacred mysteries – and that if they could only discover this magic missing something they would somehow share the secret of Creation itself. That's what the gold stood for, Gerard. Not yellow metal for buying and selling. But perfection, the elixir of life itself.'

'Do you think they were right? Or were they mad? Was Thomas Noone a bit mad?' asked Gerard, remembering that burning blue gaze.

Caroline gave a helpless shrug, and briefly bit at her lip, not quite laughing. 'Gerard you ask the most dreadful questions. I don't know how to answer you. Will would tell you that the alchemists were heroic madmen. There was one lovely one who made himself a pair of wings and tried to fly to France from the top of a tower somewhere in Scotland. He fell and broke his leg but put his failure down to the pennypinching use of chicken rather than eagle feathers. Yes, I'm sure some of them were completely mad. I think Thomas Noone was a little mad for a time. In fact I'm sure he was. He became blind to everything but his search and

95

I'm afraid that kind of obsessiveness doesn't really seem heroic to me, because whatever brilliant results it achieves by its single-mindedness, in the end it shuts out human love.' She looked away. 'And that's a kind of murder.'

'But everyone he loved had already died,' said Gerard, puzzled. 'There wasn't anyone left to shut out. You don't think probably it was just his way of not going even madder? To have something spectacular like that to dream of. Something to hope for.'

'No,' said Caroline awkwardly. 'You're right, of course – ' and she might have said something more. But just then Laurie began to cough, a hacking harsh sea-lion's bark of a cough and Caroline was up from the table in a flash, hunting for Laurie's inhaler, worrying aloud if she should make him an appointment at the evening surgery just to be on the safe side.

Laurie began to look frightened, wheezing heavily into a mansize tissue whilst Caroline questioned him agitatedly about what he had been doing that morning.

Finally, guiltily, Flora crept up to her mother and confessed: 'Mrs Krake gave him a sweet and Laurie ate it. A yellow one.'

'Oh no – Tartrazine,' wailed Caroline. 'Oh Laurie, you naughty boy. You know you mustn't accept sweets from people. If you don't want to seem rude you can just put them in your pocket and give them to me later. And Mrs Krake should know better. She really should. I've explained often enough.'

'Laurie and me can't have chemical additives,' said Flora to Gerard very gravely, gazing at him out of eyes like enormous blue pansies. 'Or eggs or dairy products or gluten. We're on a special diet.'

'And we're allergic to animal fur and house dust and pollen,' said Laurie importantly in his growly voice. 'We get ill a lot.' He blew his small snub nose with a surprisingly loud trumpeting sound. 'I'm sorry I forgot about the sweet, Mummy. I just ate it before I thought.'

'You didn't, fibber,' said Flora at once. 'You just ate it because Mrs Krake said E numbers were a lot of rubbish and you didn't want her to laugh at you.'

Gerard thought they were the most elderly small children he had met in his life. He bet they could read already. They had probably taught themselves out of a medical dictionary. He wondered how they would ever survive going to school. The other kids would murder them. Probably just by breathing on them.

Yet he couldn't help feeling a kind of admiration for them. They had a sturdy courage in the face of constant discomforts which made him warm to them. On impulse he said, 'Are there any games you like to play? I'll play with you when we've finished lunch, if you like.'

Picture Lotto, he thought, remembering the little kids passing through Deben House: Dominoes, Stickle Bricks and Mr Potato Head.

'Twins, how lovely!' said Caroline at once. 'Gerard can help you with the mathematical model book that Daddy bought you.'

And before he had a chance to protest, Gerard was borne off by his little twin cousins for a stimulating afternoon of tessellating cardboard models of hexagons and dodecahedrons. Long before his time was up, a sweating Gerard was thinking longingly of Errol who could only decipher the word aeroplane because it was the longest word in his reading book.

Harriet made an appearance at the family tea time,

silently swallowing down a cup of tea and mutilating half a sandwich, all without once meeting Gerard's eye. Gerard had been feeling kinder towards her in her absence, imagining cheering scenarios in which he diplomatically put things right between them, so that he could share with her what Will had told him. But after a few minutes of what he privately termed 'the Lucretia Borgia treatment', his resolutions wavered. She really could be obnoxious when she wanted to be.

Caroline, who had been battling unsuccessfully with maternal anxiety since Harriet came glowering to the table, suddenly capitulated and reached out towards her daughter to touch her exotically gloved hand, asking gently, 'Are you sure you feel all right?'

'Fine, thanks,' said Harriet in an ominous tone, snatching her hand out of range and nursing it as if it had been scalded.

'You're not upset about anything?'

At this Harriet leapt to her feet, knocking against the table and spilling tea, shouting, 'Can't you ever leave me alone? Why must there always be something wrong with people, Mummy? Do you know you only notice people when there's something wrong with them? If I wanted you to notice me when I was little all I had to do was fake a stomach ache or tell you someone had called me a dirty nig-nog at school. Then you were all over me. Why don't you ever try noticing me when I'm perfectly all right – just for a change?'

And she slammed out.

Everyone was effectively silenced. Caroline mopped up the tea and poured herself out another cup with a slightly shaking hand. Then Avery, silent until now, said tightly that he was sorry but he, at least, had to work, besides it was impossible to enjoy a civilised meal when other people had so little control and such minimal consideration for others. He was just stalking off to his study when he noticed something.

'What is this doing here?' he asked in that quiet voice which is worse than a yell.

He was holding up a book that had been lying on the dresser.

Along its spine Gerard could read the title: *Wholeness and the Implicate Order*. On its front cover was a dried-on, rather gluey looking trickle of something. The atmosphere plummeted. Gerard's stomach lurched in sympathy for his aunt as she said, 'Oh, Avery, I borrowed it to hold something down while I was making something with Flora. Is it important?'

'It's effectively ruined,' said Avery from somewhere beyond Alpha Centauri. 'Yes. But I suppose that isn't important to you.'

'Oh, darling,' exclaimed Caroline humorously, apparently still painfully determined, for Gerard's sake, to pretend her husband was a human being. 'Of course it isn't ruined. It's covered in perspex, look. I'm sure it will wipe off. It's only school glue or something equally innocent.' She reached out to take it from him, placatingly but he whisked it high out of reach.

'Isn't any room in this expensive mausoleum safe from sticky-fingered brats, making pointless objects out of a nightmare infinity of egg boxes and toilet rolls! Don't answer me! You don't have to. Everyone in this house believes they have the perfect right to use my possessions exactly as they please. No one respects my privacy. No one asks. No one apologises – '

Temporarily out of vocabulary, Avery stood breathing fast. Being angry should have made him more human, more approachable. But Gerard thought he remained as sealed and remote in his rage as he had been in his indifference. He had reached for a different script, that was all. Remembering the little boy with the boat, laughing, screwing up his eyes against the sun, Gerard felt the ache coming back into his throat. *It was a happy house in the beginning.*

As Avery opened the door into the hall and swept through, slamming it behind him, Gerard carefully kept his eyes fixed on his plate. If he were Caroline he would throw something at his uncle, or empty the teapot over his head, but he would bet anything that if he risked looking at her now she would be struggling to preserve her gentle smiling composure. The worse they all behaved, the harder poor guilty Caroline strove for perfect family harmony. Didn't she realise that she couldn't do it all by herself, he thought. It was like trying to row with one oar.

'Please, will you read us a story?' asked Flora, unexpectedly appearing at his elbow, tugging at his sleeve. Her lip trembled as if all the bad temper had frightened her.

'Why, what's your favourite book?' asked Gerard cautiously. '*The Encyclopaedia Brittanica*?'

'No,' said Laurie at once. 'Why – is that good? Me and Flora like *Mike Mulligan and his Steam Shovel* and stuff like that. And Flora likes fairy stories but I think they're really silly.'

Gerard went off with the twins to their cheerfully decorated bedroom. When he sat down with them on one of the fat coloured cushions scattered around the snakes-and-ladders patterned floor and started to read, he could only just hear himself through Laurie's wheezes.

'Shouldn't you take another swig out of your death ray thingy?' he suggested.

Laurie thought this extremely funny and took a while to sober down enough to return to the adventures of Mike Mulligan. Caroline came in when they had moved on to *The Tiger Who Came to Tea* and put immaculate ironing away in immaculate stripped pine cupboards. She smiled at the amicable threesome and said, 'How's your wheezes, sweetie?'

'Better after I used the death ray,' shrieked Laurie going off into even more life-endangering paroxysms when he saw the expression on his mother's face.

'Calm down,' said Gerard. 'It's my fault,' he said to Caroline. 'Sorry.'

'Best medicine,' she assured him. 'Don't worry. I think I was right not to bother the doctor.'

But she still looked worried as she went out.

'Now read this one,' ordered Flora pushing another paperback at Gerard. This was one he knew: *The Man Whose Mother was a Pirate*. He read it with as much dramatic emphasis as he could muster, surprised to find how much he was enjoying himself, and then turned to the twins' bookshelves to find something else.

'Read this – Read this!' shouted Laurie waving something. He was getting tired and shrill, a warning sign Gerard recognised from Deben House.

'I'll choose the last one,' he said firmly. 'A sleepy bedtime one.'

He poked around amongst the books finding one with its spine turned to the back of the shelf. 'Oh this is great. Errol used to like this. *The Owl Who was Afraid of the Dark*,' he said, settling back on his cushion.

But Laurie had gone rigid with alarm, as though Gerard had offered him a poisonous snake. When he could move he seized the book from Gerard with a shaking hand, flinging it into the corner of the room.

'Don't, don't you read that horrible book,' he choked, hardly able to speak through the fit of violent coughing that suddenly seized him.

'Laurie's afraid of owls,' said Flora gently in Gerard's ear, her breath tickling.

'I'm not – I'm not – it's a stupid horrible book. Take it out! Take it out of here!'

Laurie's voice was rising like a siren. He was fighting for breath. Caroline came running.

'What's the matter, chicken? What's the matter?'

'It's my fault,' said Gerard, pale. He showed her the book lying on the floor.

'Oh, lord, I thought I'd taken that out of their room,' said his aunt. 'Poor Gerard, you weren't to know. Don't blame yourself.'

But Gerard couldn't help it. How had he so quickly forgotten Harriet's words about the nightmare owl? As he slipped out of the room, almost in tears himself with guilt and distress, he heard Laurie sobbing in terror, 'Don't let it come. Oh, Mummy, don't let it come and take the light.'

9

The First Rule

When Gerard snapped on the wall switch, he again experienced that sense of faint unease, as if he had come insensitively barging in upon some grieving person's solitude. The room was empty of course. There was no one silently curled up on the window seat staring out into the darkness. He should have got accustomed by now to the way the shadows fell. But a feeling of unhappiness lingered, leaving a lonely aftertrace in the air.

He was tired. He really needed to go to bed. But somehow he felt too rotten to settle. He found himself wandering around, compulsively touching things, pushing paperbacks to the back of the bookshelf, aimlessly opening drawers and shutting them again, running his fingers over the lamplit surfaces. It was like being a small anxious child again, adrift in yet another new foster home, needing to touch everything in the room once at least to prove it was real.

But he was no longer a small child. He was no longer a passive passenger. He was Lindsey's son and, like her, he made things happen. He could choose.

In his pocket, inside his curled palm, was her talisman, the message that seemed still to be travelling myseriously towards him like light, through time and space. And though he still couldn't know whether it

103

contained the answer to his questions, or if it was itself a question he would have to answer, Gerard knew now in his heart that it was a token of her love. Somehow, for reasons that were not clear to him, like a lodestone seeking north, the small bone bobbin had brought him back home to Owlcote where he belonged.

He realised all at once that the painful feelings of the last few days had precious little to do with belonging or not belonging. Belonging went deeper than feeling safe or comfortable or simply fitting in.

'Do you know what the First Rule is?' Norah once said to him, joking on the outside but deadly serious on the inside. 'The First Rule is that you always tackle the thing that's in front of you, because the thing that's right in front of you is yours. And if you don't deal with it the first time, you'll be prevented from getting on with the rest of your life until you do deal with it.'

She made it sound as if each person was responsible for being the hero of their own life, and as if life itself was like one of those adventure games, each one unfolding a Persian-carpet pattern of gifts and curses, helpful beings, magicians to outwit or win over, mountains to scale and treasures to find.

'And this is mine,' said Gerard to himself. 'Norah's Ark instead of parents. A ruined house full of dreams that have got a separate life of their own. A witch grandmother and her apprentice. Asthma, owls and all.'

Well, he thought, it wasn't your average humdrum life.

Now it was possible to go over to the carved wooden cupboard, open it, lift out the battered shoe box Will had given him and take it to the window seat. Then he sat for a few moments with it on his lap, his heart thudding in his ears. At last, slowly and tenderly as if some timid wild creature might be crouching inside it, he lifted the lid.

Inside were two hard-covered notebooks. The first was Will's and it looked every bit as disappointing as Will had hinted it might, mainly containing notes for a long, obscure and thoroughly gloomy poem called *An Experiment in Alchemy.*

That word again.

Gerard discovered that he was getting profoundly fed up with Thomas Noone's creepy influence on the Noones of the present day. It was as if none of the family's thoughts were their own and they all half knew it but still went on thinking them helplessly anyway. He skimmed pages impatiently. Towards the end Will seemed to have abandoned the poem in favour of a hotch-potch of facts, weird alchemical diagrams and formulae, lists of some of the stranger ingredients used in alchemy (lapis lazuli, cinnabar, quicksilver), and quotations from an old Elizabethan text about the three distinct stages of the process of alchemy.

From what Gerard could make out, the vital moment was when the seething mass of molten dross began shooting out filaments of white so pure it dazzled the eyes. Then if all was going well the alchemist would see appear within the dazzle, 'all the colours of the peacock's taile.' But if it went wrong at this point, all the white stuff went sullen, red and oily and you either had to dump in a double dose of quicksilver 'to remedy the compounde' or swear, throw it all out, and start again after a good night's sleep. Beside this mildly intriguing material Will had rather perplexingly stuck in several badly typed quotations from some German-sounding psychiatrist which seemed, if possible, even more confusing than the poetry. In the end Will had obviously come to agree with Gerard because at a later date he had scrawled across the words of both alchemist and scientist in black ink:

Just putting facts together no use. Can see it with mind but not understand it with heart. Missing vital element. Finally experiment fails because no fusion. Therefore no alchemy. History repeats.

After this the remainder of the pages in the first notebook were blank.

The second notebook was older, with yellowing pages that curled. Stuck inside the cover, cut from some old exercise book was a child's handwriting: Lindsey Frances Noone, Owlcote, Saxham Parva, Rutland. The rest of her address ran on into several lines until it reached The Universe, with a great flourish. Gerard traced his fingers over it for a second, almost smiling. He liked to think of her, claiming the entire universe as her home.

But when he turned to the first page, Gerard's eyes widened with shock. For Will had written across it in his familiar black handwriting:

The Alice Books

Alice again. What could it mean? The notebook itself contained pages of gummed-in typewritten entries that seemed to have been painstakingly extracted and copied from some kind of makeshift childhood diary or series of diaries kept by Lindsey over several years. Why had Will taken such pains with what he described so dismissively as jottings and daydreams? Why had he kept the two notebooks together as though they shared a common purpose?

Who's Alice? Another cousin?

Distantly, Lark had said.

Leafing through the book with a baffled sense of loss, Gerard saw that there seemed to be nothing else in Lindsey's own hand until the last page on which Will had pasted a smudged, almost indecipherably faded child's drawing of a maze.

Gerard swallowed. Straining his eyes he could just make out a wobbly crayoned arrow pointing along the winding paths of the maze towards a sketchy little scribble of a child wearing some kind of nightdress, standing in the centre of the maze between four stylised archways. Underneath the child's scribbled starfish toes, which gave her a rather amphibious look, Lindsey had printed ALICE IS HERE underlining it several times. It was a dreadful drawing but you could tell that Alice was meant to be clutching some kind of dark bottle in her hand. And Lindsey had somehow succeeded in giving the girl an expression so starkly lost that Gerard felt physically shaken with the force of some wordless recognition. Here was something he knew. Something he had always carried deep inside. But try as he might he could not yet dredge it up into the light and name it.

There was more. Against each of the archways Lindsey had written carefully in different coloured crayons: *Earth, Water, Fire, Air* as though each represented a door into a different realm. Then bewilderingly, Will had scrawled at the top of Lindsey's drawing:

He thought the answer to the equation was perfection, Terra, Aquae, Ignis, Aeris = Aurum. *She thought it was love. They were both right and never knew it. History repeats.*

Gerard pulled at the front of his hair in frustration,

hoping vainly that physical pain might shock his dull wits into understanding. For a moment he felt like Will. He could see all the separate fragments in his mind, but not yet understand with his heart what united them. It was as if, like Thomas Noone, he had already been given everything he needed to turn his inert lump of lead into gold, but the magic still obstinately refused to work. What was still missing?

'Oh no, now you've got me binding on about gold,' he muttered aloud to the spirit of his tiresome ancestor.

He was too tired, he decided. If he didn't get some sleep first, he wouldn't be able to make sense of anything. Then tomorrow perhaps he could manage to get Harriet on her own again, and try to get through the poison barrier for long enough to convince her he wanted to help.

Unfortunately for these positive plans, just as Gerard was putting on his pyjamas, a piece of folded paper snaked itself under his door, almost giving him a heart attack.

He would have guessed it was from Harriet even if she hadn't signed it, from the distinctively violent appearance of the handwriting: all black stabbing loops that came through the other side of the paper and a great many darkly feverish swirls that turned back in upon themselves. The overall impression was of a hectic, inky curse. And so, in a way, it proved to be.

He, Gerard No one, was to forget this morning or he'd be sorrier than he'd ever been in his life. Harriet could take care of herself and she didn't need anyone else to do it for her. He'd make a pretty stupid knight errant anyway. She wasn't going to spend her life like a stunned rabbit waiting to be run over. KEEP OUT OF

MY LIFE, it concluded and this last sentence was inked over several times and underlined twice. She had signed herself confusingly HARRIET LINDANY ABDELA.

Abdela? Her African father's name?

It was too much. Whenever he decided to reach out to her, to try to make peace, she blocked him with her self-pity and melodramatics. He wished she'd be horribly smothered in the night and he needn't ever think about her again. If he thought about anything more tonight, his brain would burst.

But as he climbed into bed he found himself infuriatingly up against the common-sense truth of Norah's First Rule mingling incongruously with the memory of a handful of primroses still damp from spring woods.

Alice likes you. She thinks you might be the one.

'All right, Alice, distant cousin or whoever you are,' he said aloud, sighing, 'I got your message, second class. But the one to do what, exactly?'

And feeling himself distinctly beseiged by invisible presences, Gerard opened Lindsey's yellowing notebook at the first page and, forcing his watering eyes to stay open, he began to read.

10

The Missing Element

'It was Granddad who told me he'd seen her too,' Gerard read.

The shadows seemed to gather in upon the little circle of lamplight as though listening. As he read, his mother's words came alive for him, their tone as direct and natural as if she always knew that underneath she was talking to Gerard.

Lindsey, he discovered, increasingly unhappy and at odds with her family as she grew up, had formed a special friendship with her grandfather during his last illness, and together they shared a secret which no one else would ever acknowledge, though it had haunted the nights and poisoned the days of every single child of the Noone family for generation after generation; the story of Alice's ghost.

'They think because he's so old and weak he's just talking nonsense. Avery says he's got senile decay and it's disgusting and he won't come near him any more. I think it's not really because Granddad's disgusting he does that but because Avery's always scared when things are too real unless it's war films, then they can be as gory as they like. I said he's still the same person even if he is dying. And he doesn't talk nonsense. He's the only one of them that ever told me the truth. But I didn't say that bit. So I suppose I don't always tell the truth either. You learn not to in our house. Avery doesn't call it lying of course. He calls it being selective with information.'

Gerard, drawing renewed energy from the excitement of discovery, was now speeding through the pages, building up a kaleidoscopic impression of a private, dreamy, but inwardly rebellious child; a misfit cuckoo in a nest of Arctic eagles. But as Will said, Lindsey knew what she needed. That was why she crept off to spend precious moments with her grandfather who in turn found himself able to risk a rare new tenderness with the awkward little granddaughter he had scarcely known till now.

'Once every generation or so she picks someone to talk to and put her trust in,' her grandfather told her. 'That's you, Lindsey Noone, and don't you ever forget it. Every generation there's a chance to put it all right. April, that's her time. The cruellest month. That's when it comes round again. That's when it happened. In spring time. Spring always hurt her most. Everything growing and green and bursting open when her own life was shrinking down like a guttering candle. Winter was her heart's season and she submitted to it, you see. Obediently froze to death like a starved bird on a bough. She thought that's what he wanted. She never knew she had a choice and maybe she was right in those different times.

'The only alternative left to her was to shake her fist at them all, and the hurt he did to her; make a bonfire out of her anger and go her own way. But that would have been like choosing to be a witch and who'd freely choose that in those days? She was so afraid of what she thought she was. She always knew things that other

111

folk didn't. She heard and saw things. She had the healing gift, you know. But that frightened her too. For what good was it if she couldn't heal *him*?

'No one cared for her. She wasn't pretty. She wasn't a comfortable child to be with. Changeling, they called her. Witch brat. In the end, no one bothered if she had new clothes when she grew out of her old ones. No one bothered if she was fed. By the end she was living on sorrel and wild radishes, anything she could pull from the hedgerow.

'After she knew there was no home for her in her own time and place she began to fade. She was a ghost already in her own lifetime. Then the wild things started coming to her more and more: the birds, the deer — even a fox sought refuge in her arms once from the huntsmen crossing her father's land. Right here in the maze one sharp white winter's morning. Can't you just see it, Lindsey? The huntsmen and women in their black and gold, weighed down by their heavy furs, crashing through the hedges, murder in their hearts, their breath clouding the air. And there with the rank-smelling bright-eyed creature in her arms, defying them, the witch child, Alice Noone, her eyes as lightless as black stones. She was a hunted wild thing herself now. The creatures knew she was one of them.

'But not him. He couldn't stand to look in her face, you see, and be reminded of the others, dead and in their graves. The brilliant, beautiful sons and daughters he'd loved the best. And it was Alice who had been safely brought through the fever. Little ill-favoured Alice, pale as a shaving of bone, with her thin sandy hair and her insatiable hunger to be loved. So he turned away from the one creature in the universe that could

112

save him and shut himself away in a room that smelled of lies; hugging his darkness to himself and calling it science.'

Gerard read on, trembling with excitement. Alice the distant cousin, Alice of the primroses and the wild things, she was Thomas Noone's daughter. The only one of his family that didn't perish in the plague. The child he couldn't bring himself to love, wandering through the centuries, looking for someone who could understand. Someone who would accept her gifts and listen to her and try to befriend and save her. She had chosen Lindsey.

'Then my mother came in with his medicine and he dribbled it a bit so she had to mop him up. You can see how much she hates it because she puts on her super-efficient expression, just like Avery does when Daddy makes him carve the roast beef and it's a bit too rare. She has to pretend Granddad's some kind of object to bring herself to touch him. She couldn't come near him if she let herself think of him as human. And Granddad was being really shameless, wandering on about seeing tigers and mermaids in the garden, but that was just to throw her off the scent. He winked at me when she wasn't looking. He does hate being so helpless, but at the same time it's as if he's found a peculiar kind of freedom in it. Perhaps he doesn't feel he's got to pretend any more.'

There was a long lapse between entries after this. Almost nine months. Her grandfather had died. In April, the cruellest month. Lindsey had school troubles. Avery was a pig.

'Alice was crying again in the night. She keeps begging me to go into the maze but I'm afraid. She goes on and on about The Door and how I've got to *choose*. I think I remember something from when I was little, pretending the arches opened into different worlds, different lives. But what if I'm just imagining it? Daddy had a stern talk with me the other day. My mother must have told him to. He insisted that Granddad was completely bats in the end and that I should forget any strange stories he told me. He told me I was becoming morbid and living in the past. "Morbid" sounded like one of her words, not his. I don't know what to believe. I wish she wouldn't cry so much. I can't sleep.'

Soon after this was an entry apparently scrawled at white heat after Lindsey had quarrelled with her mother.

'*I won't believe he was mad.*

'Once he heard me singing that sad little song she sings and he explained to me that it was really an old riddle. He said the answer to it all was in there somewhere. He said he couldn't bear to think of her alone so much in this great house while her father was off chasing after rainbows and fool's gold. He said it reminded him of his own failures in the rainbow-chasing department, whatever that meant. Then he said the answer to the riddle was meant to be Man (I think he probably meant Woman as well) but Granddad said, "I think the real answer is the human child, Lindsey. Take you, for instance. All the same elements but combined uniquely every damn time. Every time a unique being with infinite potential. At the start there's no limit to what that child can do in the world. That's Creation. That's the only gold worth having. So why do we shut our eyes to it? Why don't we see what's already there? He was a bloody blind old buzzard, Thomas Noone.

Looked for the answer everywhere but where it really was, right there in the eyes of his own skinny little unloved daughter. That's the Noones all over. That's their sickness and I'm ashamed to say it's been mine until now. You've got to save yourself from it, Lindsey. You live in different times. You can make a bonfire of your anger. You can shake your fist at the lot of them. You don't have to submit and lie down in the snow and die. But if you do, all I hope is that I'm not around to be made to watch it happen all over again." I could tell he was angry with them about me when he said that. He never used to swear.

'Writing that and thinking of how he looked at me when he said it, I can't help crying, I feel so angry with her. Why can't she love me? She's my mother. The only mother I'll ever have. But when she looks at me it's as though I remind her of someone she hates. Everything I do it's the same story, even just coming into the room. As if I occupy too much space, breathe too much of her air or something. Avery says she despises me because I'm pliable and easy to push around but that's because he doesn't recognise psychological warfare when he sees it. What I do is actually quite clever because in fact nowadays I do exactly what she tells me to, exactly the way she tells me to do it. I behave perfectly. The model daughter. She can't touch me. Yet she knows it's done in total hatred of her. And every time I bring it off, I feel that much stronger than she is because I'm using her own weapons against her. But all I ever wanted in the beginning was for her to love me the way she loves Avery – ' The sentence petered out in a series of inky smudges.

There were pages more of this kind of thing. It seemed

115

as though by now the subtleties of Lindsey's struggle with her mother were consuming more and more of her energy and imagination. And the presence of Alice, the alchemists's daughter, grew fainter, almost vanishing all together only to resurface with a bang in a new startling entry which brought Gerard bolt upright in his bed.

'Chased Will round the garden with a pair of nail scissors until I caught him and made him admit he has the Owl Dream too. I know Avery had it because I used to hear him crying in the night when we were all still little. It was her dream first. Alice's. I know I have to help her. She chose me, Granddad said. I can still hear her sometimes, though I haven't seen her for months. But it isn't too late. I'm only thirteen. I've got a whole year left to try. After that it's no good, Granddad said. April's her time. If I can't manage it, it will all start happening again.

'Will said he'll never talk to me again as long as he lives. He's ashamed of what he told me. He pretends to think dreams are for little kids and neurotic women so that Avery won't laugh at him. Then he broke his own resolution, just to get back at me, and threatened to tell our mother it was me that stole the bobbin out of her room and let Avery take the blame all those years ago when we were little. I just stalked off with immense dignity and came straight up here to write this. I didn't tell him that I took the bobbin because Alice told me to. I didn't tell him I've still got it either. I did try once, when he was in an approachable mood, to tell him some of the things Granddad told me, but he became all lofty and superior and spouted on about how it was all a metaphor for a lost Eden that never was, lost paradise or something and that growing old *was*

116

pathetic but Granddad had had his day and couldn't expect to live our lives for us as well as his own.

'I got the bobbin out of its hiding place after I came up here and looked at it. I wish I could understand what Alice meant about it. I seemed to understand her so much better when I was little. I can't remember what she told me properly. Things keep getting in the way. I keep thinking that somehow, if I can just hang on to it, it'll somehow get me out of this place.'

The next entries were all preoccupied with monotonous troubles at school. Then came the incident Will had described, the accompanying family drama and the announcement that she was to be sent away.

After that there were only two more entries; the first dated several months later, during a school holiday said: 'Since I've been back at Owlcote I've tried to get Alice to talk to me the way she used to but she's gone. I just can't reach her. That's what Granddad said would happen. That means it will all go on happening over and over again. She trusted me. But all I can do now is save myself. One day I shall get away from here and it will be forever.'

The final entry in smaller, loopier handwriting said: 'I've been sitting here all day in my old romantic tower, re-reading these old diaries, laughing and crying at myself. What a goose I was. What a dreamer. But I haven't outgrown my silliness completely. When I leave tomorrow the bobbin is going with me. You have to take what you need to survive. I can't breathe here. I never could. There was always a missing element in this house, but it wasn't anything the slightest bit mysterious. Love was all it was. And now I've found it. I've become a thief for love and I don't regret it. Peter makes up for everything. He's all the world I'll ever need from now on. I've stopped fretting away at the past as if I could reverse it single-handed. If you're strong enough you can shut the door on it, cut yourself off from it forever and make a new beginning – ' The last sentence broke off as if she had been interrupted. There was nothing more.

Gerard was not in the least tired now. He felt light and cleansed all over. It was as if he had tuned into some exhilarating new source of energy. And all the while he had been reading, a daring resolution was forming. He knew now without a doubt why he had come to Owlcote. Lindsey hadn't been able to finish what she'd started. She'd got some things right and some things very wrong. Perhaps every generation a Noone child came closer to healing its family. Now he had the chance to put it right for ever. Since Lindsey ran away, slamming the door of the past behind her, Alice had been alone, waiting. She'd been waiting for him to come back where he belonged.

Within the outward structure of impressive stone and timber, Thomas Noone, without knowing, had built a second hidden house; one of shifting light and darkness, of ebbing and flowing: a house of myths and dreams and inarticulate loss. That was the real alchemists's house. His true legacy, bestowed in secrecy and silence from one generation to the next.

When Lindsey left Owlcote, to make love her whole world, she only succeeded in cutting herself off from the house of timber and stone, the family of flesh and blood. But the inward life of her family still invisibly pulled and tugged at her own, like a ghostly tide. Gerard had felt it for himself that first day, and rightly feared being sucked down into it. Lindsey had probably experienced it until she died. But if you shut the door on the past as Lindsey had, to evade the pain of your knowledge, you also shut the door on ever understanding it, on ever putting it right.

Somehow the Owlcote maze held the answer. He had been drawn to it from the first moment he saw it, and Alice too had seemed obsessed with it, endlessly pestering Lindsey to go there and find The Door.

It was now or never. It was April. The April he had turned fourteen. After that, Lindsey's grandfather had said it was too late. The whole cycle would begin again.

He wasn't going to make his mother's mistake of hanging about, worrying if he was suffering from delusions. He was going there now, in the dark, while no one could see him entering the forbidden maze. And he was taking the bobbin, Lindsey's stolen Gift, with him. He was going to find Alice.

11

The Night Maze

The great bolt slid silently back. Fortunately it was kept well-lubricated. Mentally he thanked the patron saint of 3-in-1 oil. Who would that be? Saint Olive, he thought, wanting to giggle a bit with nerves.

He hopped about shivering on the doorstep, putting his trainers on. The air was frosty, hurting the inside of his nose. The sky was brilliant, cloudless. He could smell woodsmoke somewhere.

Softly, he latched the massive door pulling it to behind him and stole across the whitened lawn towards the looming silhouette of the maze.

He hesitated beside the entrance to the alley of overhanging box. The stars blazed down. He felt ridiculously alone under all that vast indifference. The one place his witch grandmother had put off limits and he was heading there like a doomed homing pigeon.

He gave a last panicky look back at the house. In the west wing in a room below his own, a light gleamed faintly behind curtains. Harriet's, he thought. She was up late. Probably sticking pins in waxen images; manicuring her pet bats.

Step by step he edged into the maze.

Darkness swallowed him. As if a great magnetic door had slammed behind him, the sights and sounds of the garden were wiped out. He fumbled for his pocket torch and switched it on with shaking hands. It went out at once, as though blown out.

He had always hated the dark when he was small. Frozen to the spot, waiting for his eyes to accustom themselves, he was flooded with loneliness of a terribly old, terribly familiar kind.

It welled and welled from the pit of his stomach until there was enough of it to surge through his entire body in sickening wave after wave.

Without the use of his sight, without the faint creaks, rustles and squeaks of the night garden, there was nothing to distract Gerard from the awful things happening inside him, the desolation of loss, the raw searing sensation of being newly torn away from something or someone.

If I really was blind, he thought frantically, *I could still feel my way round.*

The thought comforted him. The space between the box hedges must be pretty narrow. He would stretch out his hand and then eventually he ought to be able to grope his way along, using the hedge as a guide. It was obvious. He'd just been too busy panicking to think of it before.

He began to edge along, his arm stretched out as far as it would reach, feeling around warily. He didn't want to smash his hand against a wall of spiteful branches. But there was nothing. It must be wider than he thought. He edged further to the right, still expecting at any moment to run his hand up against frosty box hedges. And went groping through empty air. Nothing. He leaned out even further, sick with panic. There must be a hedge. It didn't make sense. Soon he just had to feel the reassuringly solid spiky sensation of a hedge under his blindly reaching hand. But nothingness surged around him like a wave and he fell on to his knees, overbalancing.

But where he should have landed on grass or gravel, what he actually felt were tiles; plastic lino tiles reeking of chemical cleanliness.

Then he knew why he had recognised the fear. He was back in her house. Somehow when he'd entered the maze he had gone back in time. Not on some grand scale in the romantic way kids did in books, back to the Roman conquest or just in time to prevent the Fire of London or something. No – just far enough to get himself stuck all over again in the very worst time of his own short life.

He could hear her footsteps. In a minute he would hear her voice and feel her slapping pinching hands. In terror he scrambled to his feet.

Then he remembered something obvious.

I haven't gone back, not really. I've still got all my grown-up memories. This is just some sort of weird illusion and even if it wasn't she couldn't hurt me any more. I'm probably bigger than she is now. If she gave me any trouble I could just whack her back with her own rotten scrubbing brush.

Something happened. A subtle shifting within the dark spaces. The footsteps ebbed away into his memory. Secretly, shamefully he had dreaded the return of those ominous footsteps for years. Now he knew he was free of them forever.

For the first time he remembered that it was possible to look up. He lifted his face and gazed at the pattern of pulsing brilliance made by the stars. Why hadn't it occurred to him to do that before? The fact that it was possible now made him feel as if he had a grasp on things once again. And as his mind steadily cleared of terror, he began to understand what he should have guessed from the beginning. The daytime garden maze, of which Harriet had been so slighting, was not the same place as the Night Maze. Like the alchemist's houses the mazes might appear to occupy the same space but the rules were different.

He took a deep breath. This time, whatever happened, he wouldn't be taken by surprise.

He walked forward slowly, apprehensively at first and then with a growing sensation of astonished wonder.

He must be getting closer to something because suddenly he could hear voices and, rather surprisingly, smell cooking. There were two voices singing together an old music-hall song that he recognised. The fragrance wrapped itself around him like warmth itself. Like love. Apples baking.

'Daisy, Daisy give me your answer do,' sang the voices, one piping, wandering off-key.

Dazed, he wandered towards the downpouring light. The entire scene was flooded with the warm colouring of clear honey.

The small boy couldn't quite reach the table even though he was sitting on top of a precarious tower of cushions. He grasped a spoon too big for him, beating out the rhythm, opening his mouth comically wide to sing again. The woman had her back turned. Her bright brown hair was tied back with a silk scarf patterned with birds. He remembered tracing the design of it with his finger. He remembered the perfume of her hair when it was newly washed, and how sunlight brought out hidden reds and golds amongst the brown. He knew, when she turned, which plate she would be holding out with the apples cooling from the oven. It was his own special plate with the old-fashioned rose and the border of interlaced ribbons that flew out blowing on some eternal breeze. And he also knew that in a second she would accidentally burn herself on the molten apple and drop his plate, shattering it on the floor.

It was his own memory sprung alive, a memory he had lost and buried because of its power to hurt him. But still as much a part of him as the small scar under his lip where he had once split his face open on a broken flowerpot.

The woman sucked in her breath with shock and pain. The plate slipped from her hand. To Gerard watching in darkness it fell spinning down and down towards the kitchen floor forever.

It twisted and turned like a falling star.

But at last it struck the old-fashioned clay tiles with a splintering crash, gently exploding upwards again a little way and then at last coming to rest, dispersed. Broken into pieces the plate changed its nature, became cruel, menaced him. The floor was suddenly strewn with vicious daggers.

She was down on her hands and knees at once. 'Oh no, Gerry – look what I've done,' she cried.

But the little boy's wail went up like a siren. 'My plate! My plate – s'broken,' he sobbed, pointing a shaking accusing finger at her as if all his world had shattered into pieces with his beloved plate.

'Oh don't cry,' she begged. 'I'll mend it. Look – we can glue the pieces. I promise, Gerry. Oh dear, please don't cry. It's nothing that can't be mended.'

Tears rolled down her face; his mother, his own lonely mother.

'Please be a big boy, Gerry. I can't bear it if you cry. It's nothing that can't be mended.'

Then the little scene faded out, all the life draining out of it.

Gerard stood stricken, swallowing, staring at the empty space where it had been.

Don't cry. It's nothing that can't be mended.

Then he put his hand shakily into his pocket and closed it around the Gift. How could he have even imagined that he had forgotten? When all the time he had stored her living image deep inside him: carefully, indestructibly.

Nothing's lost, said a voice in the maze, though whether close at hand or simply within his own head, he couldn't tell by now. Besides, in the maze everything was inside. Nothing was really outside in the Night Maze.

He opened his palm with the Gift balanced on it. In the maze as he had guessed, the Gift too had a different nature. It shone with its own light like a small guiding star. It hummed with its own vibrant life. It quivered and shifted like a compass needle. Then, before he could save it, it spilled out of his hand like mercury and rolled away into the darkness.

As he plunged after it, cursing, he felt the faintest tugging and simultaneously a kind of fine tingling singing tension in his hand. He was not empty-handed after all. The Gift was guiding him. He was clutching the end of a length of thread so gossamer-fine that it couldn't be seen at all, yet as the Gift sped glimmering away into the gloom he was drawn steadily after it;

125

safely, securely but inexorably. It knew where it was taking him, he thought.

He tried not to pay attention to the scenes flowing like coloured smoke past and around him in the maze. But occasionally he saw strange and startling things: a pretty, sulky-looking girl in an old-fashioned white dress, crying into the shoulder of a dandified young man in cricket flannels. A fox in the snow, sitting up like a dog, panting so hard it looked as if it was laughing and a skinny girl in torn, filthy clothes, who caressed its ears lovingly, though her eyes were blank and empty as a bird's. Once a troop of brightly dressed people danced past to the sound of pipes and a medieval sort of drum. And another time a small boy, seeming strangely familiar, ran past in tears, crying, 'I've looked and looked for it, Daddy, honestly but I can't find it anywhere. But she won't believe me.'

Sometimes there were odd disconnected snatches of sound as if someone was searching for the right wavelength on the radio. An old-fashioned gramophone cranking out 'Tea for Two'. A burst of information on forcing rhubarb in January. And all the while he was pursuing the invisible thread, the darkness steadily lifted around him.

Now he could hear her.

'Earth, Water, Fire, Air,' sang the small blank voice.

But while the thread was tingling and singing in his hand, invisibly unwinding and drawing him on, other children were gathering around him, pressing in upon him and following behind him, as though compelled. It did seem to Gerard that he knew one, a little boy with a shadowy design of leaves upon his face and limbs. But when the child plucked bravely at his sleeve, all Gerard

126

felt was the faintest collision against his body of falling leaf, brushing moth's wing.

The expression in the children's eyes made him shiver. It was all he could do not to push them away. But he knew he must not. They were frightened enough already.

And still the Gift drew him on and still he followed and still the flickering ghostly children followed after. It was partly their colour that made them look so otherworldly, a faintly bruised-looking greenish blue as if they had become accustomed to living underwater and were permanently cold; a lost amphibious tribe.

Children who got left behind in the maze, he thought. *Like Alice.*

But he did not know how he knew.

Now the darkness changed, no longer darkness and not yet light but more like a thick swirling fog or mist. The invisible thread which had been flying along smoothly between his fingers began to catch and snag. He was arriving at last. But where?

Then something loomed out of the fog. Simultaneously, at his feet, he saw the bobbin gleaming in the grass. When he bent to pick it up the children stopped moving too and for a moment, waited, gazing at him, with fixed expressions of yearning. Then they fell back, dissolving into the fog like coloured inks on a blotter.

Then the fog itself dissolved.

Dazzled, shading his eyes, Gerard found himself alone at the heart of the Night Maze between four vast arching doorways. Light was streaming, not just through the doors but from the doors themselves. It hurt to look at them.

Long ago as a tiny child he had stood for the first

time at the shining edge of the sea, stunned at the immensity of this heaving, salt-reeking *living* thing. This memory was the closest his mind could yet take him to this new boundlessness.

And something was wrong. He struggled unhappily to identify it. He had faithfully followed the Gift. The Gift had brought him as far as it could. Why wasn't that enough? Why had it brought him so far only to cast him like flotsam upon this immense shining wasteland of silence that seemed to listen and gather understanding to itself, break in all directions like waves, then flow back.

It knew Gerard, even expected and welcomed him.

But it was waiting for, wanting something, no *someone* more.

All at once he simultaneously saw, felt and heard its question hang trembling in the air, like a dragonfly with wings of light.

Where is she? Where is she? Where is she? and then:

She has to come. She has to choose. She has to choose.

He knew at once who they meant; what mistake he had made. But he couldn't answer because it was no good. He had come charging out into the night to be a hero and he'd got it completely wrong. Harriet's note just about summed it up. Some knight errant, plunging off to the rescue. Remembering his previous exhilaration, he cringed for himself.

'Gerard No one,' he whispered.

He looked around him, his mouth drying. He had never felt so small. It was not only that the arching doors were so massive that they seemed built for a race of giants but that they challenged the very limits of what he could imagine. It was hard enough just trying to look at them properly. Their perspective shifted, and shimmered teasingly as if playing with him.

Sometimes, the doors zoomed up close enough to touch, going unnervingly out of focus as his vision blurred. Then seconds later, comet-like, they went streaking off again and immense distances, green and watery, brilliantly blue and star-strewn or tawny and quivering with desert heat stretched themselves between them and him.

But he knew they could not be touched or measured however close they came. He knew them for what they were. The same doors that Lindsey had so painstakingly crayoned when she could still understand Alice, in the days before she forgot the true meaning of what she had drawn. The Doors of Earth, Fire, Water, Air.

But it was no use, coming alone. He understood that perfectly now. Standing in the living heart of the maze, was like it must have been to stand at the dawn of the world. A time before guilt or secrets or muddle. A time before the universe scattered itself through infinity like a cosmic jigsaw puzzle.

Here it was still; round and perfect as a robin's egg.

Gerard now recognised as clearly as if someone had bawled in his ear, that the Owlcote curse sprang from the terrible mistake of a man who cut himself off in rage and terror from the living world, and took flight into a glittering frozen dream of the world as he longed for it to be. That same crippling loneliness poisoned the lives of the present day Noones like a dark subterranean river.

Each of the Noones was alone and had always been

alone. Blighted like buds by early snows before the sun could coax them open.

For hundreds of years; a succession of lonely children, one by one, curled on the window seat, staring out, dreaming alone, secretly longing for someone to listen and share what she knew before it was too late; before she forgot and became like all the others. Alice, Lindsey, Harriet. And how many unknown others in between? The real living child always left behind in the maze. The damaged half children, the halves who let themselves be confused, shamed or forced into forgetting, sent out into the world.

Avery, he thought suddenly, his skin turning to goose-flesh. It was Avery who touched my sleeve in the maze. And before that it was Avery, running past me, crying. Who will be next to join the tribe of lost children forever?

But he knew. He knew and he couldn't bear it. It was too much knowledge for one person to carry. It was like looking at Will's posters of starving African children and knowing there was nothing he could possibly do alone that could ever put it right. Paradise lost. Paradise smashed into a trillion pieces. *Don't cry. It's nothing that can't be mended.*

He had to go back and talk to Harriet. He had to try to get her to listen to him and he would have to learn to listen to her. Together it might at least be possible to try.

As this new resolution sank in, the Doors of the Elements abruptly stopped their distracting zooming and counter-zooming and stabilised themselves at a kind of compromise middle distance. At the same time they quickened to a many times intensified life, shooting out rainbow-coloured light in great exuberant fountains.

Further off, there came a faint rip of thunder like an old sheet tearing, and a distant flickering in violet air.

He could smell rain coming; felt the first pattering drops.

Simultaneously, Gerard became aware of a thrilling melodic vibration, a kind of wordless song, except that it was singing of such inhuman beauty it hurt.

Before he knew it tears were running down his face. The song seemed to have found its way into his heart and his heart was filling up with too much light so that the light overflowed into tears.

It was all there.

Behind each Door. For just one moment he had glimpsed it. All still there like an undiscovered planet. Still there, the living building blocks of earth and air, fire and water from which Thomas Noone had built his house, his maze, his life and dreams. Waiting to be released, renewed, transformed.

The singing was moving outward from his heart into the cells of his body, like light into leaves, dissolving the boundaries between his body and the singing vibrant maze . . .

His body shed its illusion of solidness, blurring, becoming a body of light and only light, constellated impulses of light . . .

With a terrifying whoosh of energy he was hurtling through time and space . . .

Then, with the dazed impression of having crashed with tremendous force through a barrier of some kind, he half-woke to find himself in his own bed.

Realising he still had on his outdoor clothes he

shuffled them off in vague surprise. Allowing himself to be sucked down again into oblivion he thought someone was saying something to him. He didn't know if it was Lark or Alice, or even Lindsey. But he had already gone too far away to hear what it was.

12

No Heroes No Black Princesses

But Harriet was making plans of her own. She was furious with herself for even trying to explain things to Gerard. She had to do it all alone. She had always known that, deep inside. She was alone and she had always been alone since the day she was left behind in a little perspex cot in the intensive care ward. She was stupid to have imagined that such an essential thing about a person could ever be changed. It was always the same. The more they knew about you, the closer you let them get, the more harm they could do.

As her thoughts beat this way and that in her head, like fire in a locked room, her gloved fingers were busily knotting strips of cloth.

It was funny when you really thought about it: funny to be rescuing yourself. When she was small she'd always loved the story of Rapunzel, imagining letting down her long long hair so the prince could climb up and fall in love with her. But it took away all your own strength, waiting; waiting in towers of your own making. It would be something, wouldn't it, to rescue yourself? To climb down out of the tower on a magic rope you had woven out of your own hair, your own self, your own dreams and longings.

But was it possible?

It seemed so unfair that the wild contradictory old stories should still keep their hold over her, like the devil having all the best tunes. Why did she still feel as if they contained some ancient hidden message. A message she had got to fathom for her very survival.

Rapunzel, Rapunzel, let down your hair, cried the witch . . .

For a moment she looked up, catching sight of her own strained watchful face in the mirror of her dressing table and her own hair plaited behind her head in as fierce and uncompromising a style as she could make it.

'But if you hate your hair so much, Harriet,' Caroline wailed, 'why won't you let me take you to have it cut nicely? Or if you wanted, I could try to learn how to plait it properly for you, with ethnic beads and things.'

Ethnic beads and things. Harriet shuddered. Caroline didn't understand anything. Not anything at all.

When Harriet was in the Infants, Caroline kept her hair short and fluffy. It made her look even sweeter of course. Sweet little pale brown girl with a halo of soft black curls like a dandelion clock standing out all round her head. The other children liked to pat it and see it spring back. She didn't mind it then. She was the only black child in the village school and had curiosity status. They all wanted to know what Africa was like. They were only little country kids. Most of them had never been further than Stamford or maybe Oakham. None of them had even been to Leicester and seen the black and Asian people in the streets, in the shops and parks. She used to make up stories for them about Africa because she felt vaguely guilty that she didn't really know, couldn't actually remember this important part of her life that made sense of her specialness, her difference from the local children. She made up stories for them about the magic Africa she carried in her head. She enjoyed telling them. She put in everything she could think of. Parrots like fire. Forests of ebony. Cities of gold.

Harriet's gloved fingers were still knotting away. The rope was growing.

Then, in the Juniors, there was a supply teacher: Miss Branch. She was thin and driven, with a voice like ice breaking under your feet. The class became uneasy, quarrelsome. Miss Branch tore up Nathan's sum book and told him to go back among the babies because he would never be anything but a great big baby. She refused to let Rachel go to the toilet and then made her stand all morning in front of the class in her wet shameful things.

But Harriet was quick and clever and she saw at once that Miss Branch was slightly mad and must not be allowed to hurt more people than Harriet could help. She watched Miss Branch carefully so that she could be sure to be always be one step ahead. So she helped Nathan with his divisions and she gave Rachel her own gym knickers to wear. And at playtime she told them stories about the cities of gold.

Miss Branch saw what Harriet was up to and it was not long before she began to single Harriet out for small subtle humiliations. Harriet put up her chin and made herself impervious. But after several weeks of it, one art lesson, she was all at once possessed by a fierce necessity that coloured the room a dull flaring crimson. Furiously, almost blindly, she covered her sugar paper with flying daubs of poster paint. When she looked up at last, the room had resumed its normal colour and she found herself the exhausted creator of an enormous erupting volcano; in its centre, a little, burning, frantically gesturing figure that was recognisably Miss Branch.

When Miss Branch saw the painting she flushed all the way down into her blouse with sympathetic heat.

But after this Harriet discovered that the punishment for playing with fire was invisibility. Miss Branch zeroed her. She simply rubbed her out like a wrong sum. When Harriet shot up her hand smartly, calling out the right answer, Miss Branch said sweetly, 'Well done, Louise.' When Harriet wrote a beautiful long poem about Africa, Miss Branch lost it and read out one Nathan had written about a dead cat instead.

After a while the other children understood that Miss Branch hated Harriet and, because they were afraid of their teacher, they began to hate Harriet too.

One day they were choosing people for the school play. Harriet was pinching herself under the table with wanting so badly to be the beautiful princess. Caroline was always telling her she was beautiful. My beautiful princess, she would say, combing out the painful tangles in Harriet's hair, which was much longer now.

Mr. Lewis, the deputy head, smiled at Harriet and told her she was going to play the princess. Harriet started to smile too. But Louise shouted: 'A black princess, sir! Don't be daft, sir. Princesses can't be black, sir.' And all the other children laughed at him for not knowing something that seemed so obvious now it had been said out loud.

Harriet's smile froze. She put up her chin. She told Mr Lewis she'd rather just be a page, thank you. When she got home she said listlessly to Caroline, 'I didn't remember princesses can't be black. That was stupid, wasn't it?'

The rope was nearly finished. Rapunzel wasn't black. Nor was Cinderella. Snow White at least made no bones about it.

Piecing together some of the story with almost no help from Harriet, Caroline was furious. She and Avery took her away and put her in a private day school where the teachers were paid to make sure that children couldn't accidentally become invisible.

But something had happened. Something had died inside her. And she couldn't tell anyone. What was the point? Who could help? Who would understand? She was alone, imprisoned with nothing but her strangeness, her oddity. But since it was now all she had, she clutched it to her all the more, cultivating it in silence. It was her only friend.

'Wouldn't you like to bring someone to tea after school?' Caroline pleaded with her, distressed for her stony-faced little daughter who was now almost always alone in her room, working furiously on her Latin and Algebra. 'Cressida seems a nice little girl.'

'No,' said Harriet. 'I don't want her. Or anyone.'

Cunning Caroline arranged for Cressida to come anyway.

Harriet threw Cressida's pretty birthday beret into the river and then ignored her all the rest of the afternoon. No one came to tea again. And soon afterwards, it seemed, Caroline was absorbed in her unexpected pregnancy, and after that in a consuming struggle for her frail twin babies' survival. It was now perfectly clear to Harriet that Avery and Caroline no longer

137

needed her as a second-best stand-in for a child of their own. They had the real thing now.

Harriet fastened the last strip. Her eyes were tired. Her fingers were sore inside their chafing gloves. She switched off her light and prised open her window. There was a distant glow in the east.

She had actually convinced herself that Gerard might be the one. Where there was a curse, she had reasoned, there might also be found the means of undoing it. Like the old fairy tales written in darkness and light. For a short crazy time she had allowed herself to hope that a long-lost cousin from nowhere might really do the trick. Despised youngest sons who nevertheless saved the kingdom. Old women who were not after all – behold – ugly old hags when they were kissed, but lovely young girls under an evil spell.

But not in my heart, she thought. In her heart she knew there were no heroes. In real life there were no magical figures who burst into your life transforming rags in a burst of stardust, just as there were no black princesses and everyone else but herself had known it. It was just that when she saw the lilac showering Gerard with its flowers she had almost been able to –

She shivered and looked down out of her window at the great gnarled branches of the pear tree below. Blossom clung still, white as sea foam; so fragile the faintest wind could unfasten it, send it scudding wildly through the air, like snow out of season.

It should reach, she thought.

Suddenly she experienced a surge of fierce triumph. 'I won't wait to be cursed,' she said aloud. 'I'm not a stunned rabbit.'

She ducked back into her room and gathered up a

138

great shapeless fur coat that had been lying beside her on the bed. She shrugged her arms into its sleeves. She took off her glasses and put them carefully into her pocket for now. Then she looked round for something dependable to tie her rope to. The bed of course. That's what they always did in stories. She threw the free end of her rope softly out of the window.

Harriet had been so absorbed in the drama of making her rope that she hadn't actually thought very clearly about what it might feel like to entrust herself to it, swinging loosely between the wall of the house and the upper branches of the pear tree.

She hesitated. Then: 'Well, why shouldn't it be strong enough,' she said angrily.

As the sky turned faintly rose over the park, Harriet let herself out of her window and climbed slowly and carefully down the rope into the giant pear tree. When she was safely positioned in its great cradling boughs she sighed, a deep exhausted sigh, knowing that something momentous was finished, as if she had twisted and plaited together in her rope, something more than torn-up cotton rags, as if she had somehow begun work on something quite new. So new it was not yet ready to speak or show itself. Leaning her back against the broad gnarled bark, she watched the rest of the dawn come up.

She was safe from them all for a while at least. The pear tree had no accessible lower branches, though it must have had in Uncle Will's day, she remembered, because he had once fallen out of it playing pirates and broken his arm. She sank herself deeper into the old Oxfam fur. A chill but fairly light rain began to fall; nestled in animal furs under the sheltering leaves she scarcely felt it. She thought that at this moment she didn't much care if she died so long as she had chosen it for herself. The important thing was to have a choice. And this was the only choice she had. *Harriet Lindany Abdela*. She was not Harriet No one any more.

13

A White Dress and a Straw Hat

'*It's too late! She's gone forever!*'

Old Harriet Noone groped for the light, her heart pounding.

Damn it, why were dreams so much realer than waking life these days? It humiliated her; bursting out through the skin of sleep, like a diver surfacing, shaking and shouting aloud with fear or rage, to discover that she was not after all burning or drowning or pursued by famished beasts but lying unharmed in a quiet curtained room.

What she could never understand was why, if the feelings were so real, did the dramas that inspired them fade so rapidly from her memory, leaving only bizarre traces: a weeping child who turned to gold, an owl filling the whole screen of her vision, blotting out the light, and hauntingly, a bush starred with summer roses just out of reach beyond a burning doorway. (Indifferent to flowers in waking life, Hatty Noone longed unreasonably to plunge her face in the dusky golden cups of these dream roses. But she was always too frightened of the heat of the flames to pass under the arch.)

The senseless anger and dread of a moment before,

still boiled in her blood, and hammered in her ears. But why? Her hands were clenched on the pillow, she saw, the knuckles white. In the dream she had wanted to hit and hurt someone for letting it happen. But who and what? All she could remember now was storming into the old maze to punish someone, angrily following the taunting echoes of children's voices down dusty pathways, but when she reached the centre there was nothing there but an empty antique birdcage, its door swinging open, mocking her.

And now inexplicably her head was full of Lindsey.

It was his fault. That child. The boy Avery and Caroline had brought back to Owlcote to torment her, to destroy what little peace and rest she had left to her. The boy had eyes the image of hers. How could she be dead and her eyes still live on in an unknown child? How could she be dead and her expression still look out from a pale wary face, hostile, judging?

The things Lindsey said when she left – as if an old wound had been ripped open in the air between them and all the dark poison come gushing out in a river of words. She was ill for days, trying to shut out the memory, trying not to hear. Lindsey was such a gentle biddable child to begin with. Hatty had rather despised her. But then she had known that a daughter would be a disappointment. It was Avery she had loved from the first. The son who would go out into the world as a man and be free and fight her enemies for her. He would be strong where she had been weak and return to lay his trophies in her lap. Her prizes. All hers, at last. Avery was to be perfect as she had never been, and into him, her firstborn, she poured all her scalding pent-up dreams.

But what had it come to in the end? One dead and the other gone so far from her it was like talking to someone on a distant planet. And William. William was simply weak and helpless, an amiable fool like his father; with his Save the Otter, Save the Unicorn. His epic poems. His organic apple juice. He was still a great soft child, afraid to go out into the world like a real man should and earn some proper money. Perhaps she should let that red-headed lawyer girl have him after all. What difference would it make? Recently she had lost interest in the struggle.

Suddenly she longed for Bertie to appear, blinking sleepily, and put his arms round her and pat her shoulder in his ghastly ineffectual way and tell her not to be such a silly old thing. She had never missed Bertie much before.

Painfully she pulled herself upright in the great canopied bed and found her dressing-gown on the chair where Krake had left it for her. *Krake.* Sounded like the noise an old crow might make. She was an old crow too. Hatty Noone tittered, cheering up. Don't think she hadn't seen that charming incident yesterday with peevish little Lawrence and the yellow sweet. Pure spite. Still it had amused her enormously. Caroline made such fools of her children with all her neurotic fussing, creating sickly freaks out of two and a little witch out of the other.

Sometimes she thought that girl would end up a lunatic . . .

It had felt so unnatural, bringing her into the house. She never even cried properly like a real baby, just let out those terrible screams as if she'd suddenly woken to find herself alone on a mountain ledge instead of safely in Caroline's doting arms. Little dark changeling with that angry stare. Her little fist clenched. Her mouth a screaming O that wanted to swallow the whole world into itself. She had seen at once that the child hated her.

'She always hated me,' she muttered.

Then she felt queasy and confused. For a moment the accusing image of Harriet wobbled and changed into *her*, into Lindsey. And beyond, as though in the dim interior of some half-remembered mirror, another ghostly child in a dark dripping place, screaming with terror and rage.

She shivered. She was losing her grip.

She would make herself a cup of tea and then perhaps she could get back to sleep until Krake got up and then it would be breakfast time. Her mouth watered at the thought of a meal, though when it came she would only pick at it. She was never hungry when it came to it. Never slept, never ate, never talked to anybody . . .

She moved stiffly around in the stale curtained dusk, plugging in the kettle Krake had filled for her, putting teabags in the pot. *Gerard*. What kind of name was that? Avery had been bad enough but Bertie had insisted on it in one of his rare bouts of open self-assertion. Old family name he said and that was that. But *Gerard*.

'Mousy-looking boy,' she said aloud, startling herself. Sometimes she talked aloud when she still imagined she was only thinking. To judge from Caroline's pained expression she guessed she occasionally said some rather shocking things. *But he is*, she thought again. A mousy undistinguished nothingy little boy. Probably not too bright. But then the little witch *was* bright. Sharp as a razor and nothing but trouble. She'd warned Avery of course, right at the beginning. But he was still besotted

144

with Caroline and Caroline was desperate to have a child, any child, to fill the empty space in her arms. First the little witch and now *him*. Why stop there? Why not the whole of Dr Barnardos, she wondered.

Oh let them do what they liked. They'd made it perfectly clear they didn't give a fig for her opinion any more. Just went crashing about in the minefield of the past as if it was a flower garden. As if that would put things right. As if anything ever could.

'He belongs with us,' Caroline said primly, and that was that. It was like some sort of conspiracy. She could see from the little self-satisfied looks they exchanged, how they'd all been planning it behind her back. Will and Avery looking at her all shocked and disapproving as if *she* was responsible for Lindsey's irresponsible behaviour and its consequences. As if they were nobly taking it on themselves to right the wrongs of their elders. And then they simply brought the boy out of nowhere to live here, as if she were already dead and in her coffin. As if they wished she was . . .

Hadn't Avery any heart? Had he any idea what it did to her to see Lindsey's eyes staring out of that child's peaky streetwise face? Even the way he moved his hands was hers, pushing them slyly behind his back as if he was hiding something. The lord knew where he'd been all these years and who he'd been with. With beginnings like his . . .

Everything I needed to survive I had to beg or steal. I think you even grudged me the air I breathed and the space I stood in. I used to pretend you weren't really my mother so as to explain to myself why you couldn't love me. I was a cuckoo child. Left with you by mistake. I was sure my real mother would love me if I could only

145

find my way back to her. I couldn't bear to believe the truth. That you were the only mother I was ever going to have. Do you know what you've done to me? You've made me a thief – a thief for love. You did that! You!

Tunelessly Hatty began to drone 'Tea for Two' until she could no longer hear the accusing voice; until she was left with nothing but a blurry sensation of headache that two aspirin would soon settle.

The water was boiling. She filled the teapot and then waited greedily for her cup of strong hot tea. The anticipation was the best part.

I'm like a child, she thought suddenly, catching her breath in fear. Marking empty days and nights with quarrels, mealtimes, naps and cups of tea.

Why did all her thoughts nowadays go round and round in circles. It frightened her. As if she were trapped in an endless whirlpool with no way ever to get out. Just round and round and round.

Her eyes settled on the old tin trunk. It would only make her feel worse, she knew, but she couldn't resist. She fumbled for a few minutes futilely with the catch until her fingers remembered the trick of it. Then she raised the lid softly as if afraid to surprise a sleeping self.

First the dress, still folded away between layers of tissue; no longer white and fresh as a summer rose but brittle, ivory with age. The dress she had worn the day Bertie proposed. Beside it, the straw hat with its faded rose ribbons. She picked the hat up and laid it for a moment against her cheek, forgetting about her tea . . .

Wondering where she and Theo had got to, Bertie came upon her round the corner of the maze where she stood alone, still drying her eyes; still pulling herself together, getting ready to go out and face the others in the summer garden. Bertie Noone was the last person she wanted to see. But then, as he drew closer, she had seen her fate suddenly in his widening eyes.

Of course she would marry Bertie.

She could see it all as clearly as if she was watching her own life from a great height, the appalling unfolding pattern of it, the cruel rightness of it. Of course she would not marry beautiful irresponsible Theo but Bertie, his clowning cousin, his foolish faithful shadow. Bertie had always been afraid of her until now but in her pathos, humbled, he would find her touching, approachable. She couldn't bear to see how beautiful she had suddenly become to him. She was hideous to herself if Theo no longer wanted her. Yet she knew as if it had been written in stone, that now she would turn away from love forever and marry Bertie Noone. What else could she do? Secretly she had always known she would never love and be loved. Since childhood she had woken from dreams with the tears streaming down her face, knowing the loneliness ahead of her.

So when Bertie looked at her in that quizzical lopsided way, like a puppy with one ear up, when he seemed to believe he could comfort her, and even, against all the odds, that she could comfort him for his own life's shortcomings, she thought, well, if Bertie can't tell the difference between love and this poor second-hand thing, he deserves to be made miserable for the rest of his life. But at least I'll have Owlcote. *And I'll be safe*.

There were green leaves unfolding, the smell of roses. Dusk was falling as they walked out of the maze, hand in hand and someone was playing 'Tea for Two' on a scratchy wind-up gramophone.

At the end of his life Bertie had got some sort of obsession about the maze. Said something terrible had happened to him there. But if you were ever foolish enough to ask him what, you couldn't get any sense out of him at all. She'd humoured him, of course. No one went there now. She had nothing to reproach herself with. She had nursed both his parents through their final illnesses. The old man had been difficult, senile towards the end and formed an unhealthy friendship with Lindsey, encouraging her defiance, her waywardness. There had been difficult times. But Hatty had always done what was right. She believed she had been a good enough wife to him. Given Owlcote an heir. They'd understood each other as well as any other couple . . . But if there was a God, if she ever met Him, she would just like to ask Him what the blinding blazes He meant by it? Why torture people so by letting them glimpse, even for a moment, all that glorious shining and then let it dwindle down to a handful of dust.

She let the hat fall. That wasn't what she was looking for. It was something else, something the boy had put into her head, lord knows why, with his fool questions about her birds. She rummaged around in the trunk, rejecting with a snort of disgust pictures of Bertie in the old days with his hair slicked back. No girl could have been vainer.

Then she found it. A page torn from an old newspaper, brittle and yellowed with time like her dress. Possessively she took it back to bed with her and settled down against her pillows with her steaming tea cup.

148

AMAZON EXPEDITION DEPARTS she read. She read it again. Vanished days of unmapped forests and rivers; tribes no one had ever seen. Birds the colour of fire. Cities of gold.

There was the foggy fading picture of Gus Hollyband and his travelling companions peering self-consciously at a map of South America for the convenience of the photographer. The would-be heroic report in the journalistic style of the 1930s described the intrepid well-born young explorers on the eve of their expedition to the Amazonian rain forests.

She was right. It was a mistake to look at it. Dreams should be lived on the wing or else forgotten, not shut away to turn brittle and crumble into pieces like dead butterflies.

It was just that once or twice she had imagined she saw another figure in the photograph, a ghostly girl with dark curls and a white dress. A girl who should have been with them. A girl who used, when she was twelve or thirteen, to run away to Owlcote and hide up in the old pear tree, crying and banging her bare knuckles against the bark until they bled, vowing she'd never forget how it felt to burn with a furious dream she couldn't share with anyone, never forget she was born to be free . . .

Krake would be in soon. She didn't want Krake poking her long nose into her private belongings. But she felt suddenly too tired to get out of bed again and put everything away. As furtively as any child she hid the paper inside the linen pillow slip so she could put it away later when she felt better.

Then for a long while she lay without moving in her

great airless canopied bed, old Hatty Noone, staring at nothing, her face expressionless, her eyes as empty as holes in the air. What was she seeing? Birds like fire. Cities of gold.

14

Words Fail Avery

'But she could have killed herself!' exploded Uncle Avery.

Gerard, still groggy after his night in the maze, walked unwittingly into a scene of uproar. Caroline had been crying. Laurie clutched his inhaler, wheezing away, staring around at everyone, wide-eyed. Flora, still in her nightdress and slippers, wept with continuous thin wails of terror.

'The stupid crazy girl!' shouted Uncle Avery. 'What does she think she's playing at? I'll teach her to make a fool out of me.'

He strode towards the door, slamming a chair savagely across the kitchen so that it struck the dresser, making all the cups tremble on their hooks. A plate fell off its ledge with a crash. Flora howled. But Caroline moved even quicker than her husband, catching hold of him by the back of his jacket before he could storm straight out of the kitchen.

'Make a fool of you,' she said disbelievingly. 'Is that the worse fate you can imagine – to be made a fool of?'

Gerard had noticed before what a marvellous voice Caroline had when she really chose to exploit it.

Avery was still breathing quickly but he had stopped in his tracks. 'Of course it isn't,' he said, passing a hand over his face with a look of exhausted bewilderment.

'You know it isn't. It's different for you, Carrie. You're good with words. Other people can't always find the right – formula. I don't know what to do. Shall I get a ladder from Will's place and get her down? I don't fancy risking my neck on that damn home-made rope of hers.'

At this point everyone noticed Gerard.

Laurie took a reviving swig from his inhaler, explaining gruffly, 'Harriet climbed down the old sheets into the pear tree and she doesn't want to come down.'

'But why?' asked Gerard bewildered.

Then he remembered. YOU'D MAKE A PRETTY STUPID KNIGHT ERRANT. The light burning late at night behind her curtains. This was what she'd been planning.

'I wish you'd tell us,' said Avery bitterly. 'You've been here three days. You probably know her as well as we do.' He broke off and said awkwardly to his snuffling little daughter, 'Oh Flora, don't cry, silly girl. Everything will be all right.' But he sounded helpless and Flora, uncomforted, wept on.

'Well?' said Avery to his wife. 'Shall I get the ladder?'

'I don't think so,' said Caroline. 'I think it might be wisest just to leave her where she is for a while. She can't come to much harm. She's well wrapped up and she's always had a wonderful sense of balance. She could have killed herself climbing down her stupid rope but she didn't. So perhaps we should leave her until she feels ready to come down and cope with us all again.'

'Ignore her, do you mean? Show her she can't blackmail us with her stupid adolescent tantrums?'

'I didn't quite mean that, Avery,' said Caroline sighing.

152

Watching them both Gerard realised that the trouble with his uncle and aunt was that they lived in totally different continents and each, even when they used the same words, understood an entirely different language.

Gerard could see how tired Caroline felt at the thought of being his guide and his interpreter yet again.

'It's just that she's been so miserable and bottled up for so long – and for some reason this is the way she's chosen to break out,' she said at last. 'And honestly almost anything is better than that blank angry contemptuous face of hers. Everytime I speak she looks right through me as if I was a big zero. Let's face it, I haven't been able to find a way through to her. Where Harriet's concerned I'm an abysmal failure.'

'But you're so good with people,' said Avery, astonished. 'You've always been so good with people.'

'For Heaven's sake, I'm not "good with people", Avery,' she burst out, exasperated. Then, lowering her voice, softening her expression, she went on, 'I know you're trying to be kind but it's not something I just happen to be "good" at. I try hard to understand people. I try to imagine all the time how it feels to be them. I work at it *all the time*, Avery. You don't see it but Lottie showed me – I know you don't like her, Avery, but she's been a wonderful friend to me – and Lottie says I'm like a pond snail, clamped to the walls of the family aquarium, endlessly processing everyone else's murky old water and sometimes, quite honestly, that's just what it feels like. Anyway,' she looked down, her eyes filling, her voice failing her, 'I'm not good with this particular person. She thinks I'm worse than poison. I know there was a time when she smiled into my eyes as if I was America, her new-found land or something.

But that is so long ago that I would think I'd dreamt it if I didn't have photographs of her when she was tiny.'

She glanced across at the cork pinboard. For the first time Gerard saw amongst the letters from Harriet's school, the bean collages and dentist's reminders, a colour photograph of a small pale-brown girl in a pink flowery smock and pink ribbed tights, her hair in two glistening clouds, tied back with ribbon. The little girl gazed directly out of the picture with a soft open look. It seemed impossible that it could be Harriet.

'I should have fought for her at that bloody school,' Caroline burst out suddenly, her eyes brimming. 'I've always been a lousy coward and she knows it. I didn't know how to help her. I'd been brought up in such a nice safe white world. I tried to pretend it all still was. I closed my eyes to it. I never meant to close my eyes to *her*.

'She came into our lives like a gift, an absolute gift. I think she literally saved my life. When we brought her home I was afraid to sleep. I would just lie there, hour after hour, listening to her breathing, terrified she would stop. She'd been ill for a long time before she came to us, Gerard. It took her a long time to learn to trust us – and then – '

'Do you think that if you blame yourself for everything that will make it all better?' said Avery harshly. 'I'm going to get that bloody ladder. She's not pushing me around, the little madam. She's had ev – '

'Oh please don't get the ladder,' said Gerard to his own surprise. 'She'll be all right. A girl went out on the roof once at Norah's. Phil went out, too, after a while with some sandwiches and a flask of coffee. Then after a bit they both came in again.'

154

'If you think I'm spending my valuable time climbing up and down trees with helpings of coffee and sandwiches you can damn well think again,' said Avery, comical in his horror at the very idea of such permissiveness. But Gerard could see he was simmering down. The night in the maze had changed Gerard's feelings towards his uncle. Every time he looked at him he experienced again that ghostly moth's-wing brush against his sleeve and was forced to remember a small boy with a boat, laughing, the sun in his eyes.

He could see now what had been hidden from him before, that Avery, his mother's firstborn, had grown up terrified to death of getting anything wrong in case he turned out not to be the perfect child after all. That without a borrowed script or tried and tested formula to guide him, Avery was instantly reduced to either bluster or silence. When he had to deal with this utterly ridiculous, totally unique situation: SOLICITOR'S DAUGHTER CLIMBS INTO PEAR TREE AND REFUSES TO COME DOWN, he was completely lost, having no inner maps of his own. But in the landscape of the heart there are no other kind.

'You could leave her for a while,' he suggested aloud. 'And if she doesn't look as if she plans to come down tonight I could go and sit with her for a while and talk to her.'

And get punched on the nose and thrown out on my head, he thought.

'There aren't any lower branches,' said Caroline, wiping her eyes. 'You'd either have to go up a ladder or – come down the way she did.' She shuddered, visualising it. 'But I honestly don't think I could bring myself to let you.'

She suddenly gave Gerard a good long hard look as though, momentarily, her own personal fog had cleared and she could actually really see him. 'This doesn't seem to strike you as nearly as bizarre as it does us, does it? I get the feeling you're almost at home in this kind of crisis.'

Gerard sat down at the kitchen table and edged towards the cereal bowl and the large earthenware jar that held the muesli. He was starving.

'Go on,' said Caroline. 'Poor Gerard. Please have some breakfast. I don't mean to be such a neglectful aunt.'

'It's not that I don't think it's a pretty weird thing to do,' he said, pouring himself out a generous stream. 'It's more that pretty weird things happened quite often at Norah's Ar – at Deben House. I suppose we all got rather used to it. People going through things. And then coming out of them again.'

'Well, shall I go to work? I gather the consensus is to leave her to stew in her own juice for a few more hours,' said Avery, still vainly groping for some form of words, fully guaranteed against fire and flood, which would protect him from having to *experience* this dreadful morning for himself.

'Please, Avery, yes, do go,' said Caroline fervently. 'We'll be perfectly fine. If we should need a man and a ladder unexpectedly we can always ask Will.'

So Avery departed for his office and Caroline helped Flora to dress herself. Then, having found a huge box of coloured buttons and beads for the twins to sort out, she went over to the sink with the kettle and began to fill it.

'Coffee, Gerard?'

'Oh yes please,' he said greedily. He had already grown to love Caroline's coffee. Yet, all too dizzily aware this morning of other wavelengths, he wondered how many selves were crowded inside his ordinary looking skin-for-one. How was it possible for him to sit comfortably spreading honey on his bread, breathing in delicious fumes of coffee beans, and simultaneously hold inside him the awareness of everything he had encountered in the Night Maze.

All at once he had a floating sensation, as if he had suddenly been lifted up to one of those high places where it's possible to see several counties on a clear day, only with Gerard it was not counties that were spread at his feet but realities. At the centre of his consciousness was his healthy hunger, the sensation of bread in his hand and mouth, and a vague awareness of the twins squabbling at his elbow. Further off Avery, baffled and lonely, was stalking towards the garage. In a wider arc still, Harriet huddled in her tree like a sullen chrysalis dreaming of summer wings.

Somewhere in her own twilight part of the house his witch grandmother was feeding her caged birds. Further beyond in time and space yet approaching so close now he could almost reach out and touch her, was Lindsey – yes – he could feel her, watching him, wondering.

And further off whirling helplessly within a core of darkness he could not penetrate, Alice and Thomas Noone. And all the time the Doors in the maze, shooting out their coloured fountains of light and waiting, waiting in their shining silence.

'Penny?' asked Caroline, smiling, filling his mug with coffee. 'For your thoughts? You were miles away.'

'Oh,' he said, blinking. 'I'm not sure. I think I was

157

thinking how big reality is. And how you can never get far enough above it to see the whole pattern. I mean – I used to have an imaginary friend. That's what she was supposed to be, imaginary. But to me she was just a different sort of real. I think that what people call real is mostly just official reality. But there's another unofficial sort that's much bigger and every now and then it breaks out into the official sort and shakes it up a bit.'

'And that's what people call magic,' she said seriously, sitting down opposite to him, wiping her hands on her long blue skirt and picking up her own coffee mug.

He nodded, relieved he hadn't made too much of an idiot of himself. Curiously he had only just understood about Lark, hearing his own words let loose in the air. When he first arrived at Owlcote, he had panicked, believing Lark was fading from him, that she was abandoning him, but that wasn't it at all. There was no emptiness where she had been. It was more that the boundaries were blurring. She was merging into him, no longer seeming so strange or fantastic. It was not that he had ceased to tune in to her for advice or that she had ceased to answer, but that without realising it, increasingly, he had come to think of her as just another older wiser-seeming part of himself, a part he could choose to listen to or disregard but never lose. But first his everyday reality had had to stretch to let the possibility of Lark into his life. He felt excited at this idea.

'Do you think it's possible to sort of *stretch* the official kind of reality so that it changes? So it can hold more? Become more magical?' he asked.

'Yes,' said Caroline. 'I think that has to happen before

158

any kind of change takes place. We have to be able to imagine things first or glimpse them in dreams, whether it's how to make fire, or DNA or – or space travel. If you really want my opinion, I think we need the other kind, your magic unofficial kind, just as much as we need food and water. But I used to be an actress – so I've had at least one foot in unofficial realities in my time.'

Idly she pushed some of the buttons around on the table to form a vaguely circular shape.

'Oh that explains the way you use your voice,' he said impressed. 'Did you do a lot of acting?'

'Not really,' she said apologetically as if he would now think less of her. 'Mainly walk-on parts and months and months out of work or cooking lunches for business executives in between. I did once do a commercial for Neptune's frozen fish pie. I was a mermaid.' She began to giggle, remembering it. 'In the end it seemed more dignified to be *making* fish pie, rather than flitting around Neptune's plastic palace trying to smile, swim and swallow at the same time.'

'Is Lottie an actress too?' he asked. The remark about Caroline being a water snail had snagged irresistibly in his mind, like sheep's wool on wire.

She scattered her button circle and began unconsciously rearranging it into some kind of giant flower. 'No – Lottie's an artist. She lives near here. I'll take you to sample her wonderful Swiss baking some time. She's a dear friend. Fiercely independent. Not at all like me.' She broke off and then said impulsively, 'It is so nice having you here, Gerry.' Her face flushed with affection for him. 'You don't hate being called Gerry, do you? I want you to know that it feels so right having you here

– I really think you were what was missing in our lives all the time without our knowing it – '

'*Mummy!*' growled Laurie, grabbing back a handful of his stash of buttons.

'Sorry, darling, did I spoil your lovely pattern?'

'Of course not. I wasn't making a stupid pattern. I was being a gambler at a casino and those were my chips.'

Gerard, who had turned slightly pink, grinned down at his cereal bowl. Trust him. He couldn't quite believe he had heard her correctly. *She liked him.* Not because he was a Noone and she was supposed to, but because he was himself. Her unexpected offering started to work in him like the granules of some invisible but powerfully active yeast. If he didn't watch out he would puff up to three times his original size right where he sat, like a batch of proving bread dough.

But Caroline was on her feet again, pacing and peering through her kitchen window though she couldn't possibly see anything much through it, worrying about Harriet. 'This is so awful,' she muttered. 'What a long day it's going to seem if she doesn't come down. Oh I wish, I wish that there was something I could do.'

15

Song Without Words

Time passed in the pear tree. Harriet proved unshakably deaf to her father's shouts and her mother's pleas and after a while everyone went away.

Some time later the twins came to stand underneath her, staring upwards in puzzled awe: two stern little gnomes in identical hooded duffles and red wellingtons. As they went trudging back to the house, Harriet heard Laurie say gruffly, 'She'll have to come down some time. When she needs a pee.' And Flora went off into one of her high-pitched giggles.

Strange as it might seem to more rational souls, until this remark, Harriet had not once considered the needs of her bladder. She stifled a twinge of alarm. It shouldn't bother her for a while. She prided herself on her self-control. She had even stopped herself dreaming when a spate of nightmares threatened to extend their influence into waking as well as sleeping hours. Without self-discipline, Harriet considered, one was little better than blancmange. She despised bodies and their continual puppy-like whingeing for attention and comfort. She would think of the holy men who allowed themselves to be buried alive only to be dug out weeks later, cheerful as crickets and in splendid good health. She would think of the shamans who pierced themselves with nails and commanded their flesh not to bleed.

She thought of them. But she wished Laurie hadn't mentioned peeing all the same.

As time passed in the pear tree, nestled in her shabby furs, Harriet felt increasingly warm and protected. As the morning wore on and no one else appeared to order her to come down and behave like a normal adolescent and be nice to her mother, she began to relax; to enjoy the soft movement of the air against her cheek and hair, the complex whispering of the leaves.

Gradually, a dreamy, contented sensation stole over her and once, without knowing beforehand what she was going to do, she found herself stretching out her gloved hand and stroking the mouldering bark as if it were a living creature. Loosening blossoms settled in her hair. She could see the hard green swellings of budding baby pears. It seemed to her in her solitude that in some curious way the pear tree recognised her, acknowledging, even accepting her presence.

Lunchtime came and went, or so she supposed, having no watch, and still no one came near. The afternoon continued as gently grey-green as the morning though she sensed an alteration in the quality of the light. She didn't feel lonely. In a way she felt less lonely up here than she did in her mother's too warm, too intimate kitchen.

She certainly didn't miss her lunch. In Harriet's opinion people thought far too much about food. Planning it, shopping for it, cooking and washing up after it. Then dieting because they'd eaten too much. Endless senseless activity that just got in the way of all the things that really mattered.

All right, Miss Know-it-all, said the sour quarrelsome

162

voice that lived inside her head. *And what are the things that really matter?*

'This,' said Harriet at once, and out loud, to her own extreme surprise. And with gathering certainty. 'This. Just being alive. Like this.'

Perched amongst the incessant green motion of the leaves she felt a sudden rush of delight that almost frightened her. *Up here, I really am alive*, she thought.

And at that moment she felt a sympathetic pulse under her hand.

'And you're alive too,' she whispered. 'I know you are. All this time you've been listening to my thoughts. You've just been waiting for me to notice you. You even – almost – like me.'

And again there came that quick tingling current under her hand, tangible to Harriet even through the knitted fibres of her glove.

She became utterly still. Something extraordinary was happening to her and she was terrified to ruin it by making an ugly movement or a jarring sound. Every fibre of her being became intensely focused on maintaining this mysterious connection.

Perhaps if she could just keep listening, keep on listening in the right way, perhaps the tree would go on trusting her, opening itself to her. *Talking to me*, she thought.

Time took on a different quality. She ceased at some point to be aware of her own breathing. Boundaries blurred. There was no longer separateness, loneliness. There was no longer tree or girl. Past or future. She no longer knew what she saw with her own eyes and what the tree showed her. The world became curiously fluid as if it were restlessly seeking new alignments, new forms in which to cast itself. Sometimes the house was there and sometimes it was not but the pear tree was there always, the one still point, always broad and comforting at her back.

She wasn't always alone. A succession of ghostly girls came and went in silence among the blossoming boughs. A wild girl, thin as a paring of bone: her eyes, peering through uncombed hair, as blank as a bird in a hedge. A furious child in a grass-stained sailor dress, beating her torn and bleeding knuckles again and again upon the trunk of the pear tree. And another, secretive girl, who held something jealously clenched in her hand. Harriet realised that she knew them all as well as she knew herself. As if they had been talking to her all her life. As if they had a message for her. Or a warning.

But folded in the darkening dancing heart of the tree, Harriet had never felt more alive. From the soles of her feet to the crown of her head, her skin stung and pricked. Every cell on the surface of her skin drank in the sights and sounds of the earth like sunlight and in exchange returned her own unique energy to the earth.

A bright fuzz of light shimmered along her limbs, its intensity ebbing and flowing like invisible tides. Within her body as though part of her, she felt the presence and motion of each leaf, each budded pear, each star.

Something was wrong with her throat; a growing ache, unbearable as if something were locked behind it. Something that wanted to loosen itself, burst out, break free.

Yes, came the answering green pulse in her own body. *Yes. Don't be afraid.*

And she opened her mouth and breathed a deep breath. And found herself singing.

At first she sang old songs, silly songs, family car-journey songs, folk songs she'd forgotten she knew; snatches from musicals, scraps from *The Magic Flute* which Will had once taken her to see. She sang 'Yellow Submarine' and 'Row Row the Boat' and 'Jesu Joy of Man's Desiring'. But as the energy swelled and grew within her she became frustrated with the clumsiness of words which seemed to block and choke the flow of the music trying to find its way out of her body.

And that was when she began to sing most wildly, most beautifully at the top of her voice.

Indoors it was still only dusky late afternoon and time was passing agonising slowly for poor Caroline who could no longer suppress her anxieties.

'She can't stay there all night. Perhaps she thinks we just don't care if she gets hurt or not. Perhaps I was wrong, Gerry, not to let Avery bring her down safely. He'll be home soon and he'll be so angry if this is all still going on. He can't bear family dramas. They make him ill. Sometimes he has dreadful migraines that go on for days.'

'Let me go. Let me just try,' said Gerard. 'If it doesn't work, I'll come back and we can try something else.'

Shrugging on his awful anorak and setting off through the mild drizzle he thought that Caroline had completely misunderstood her daughter's motives. What Harriet wanted was not to harm herself but to be saved. But instead of wailing and whingeing for rescue she was trying, however improbably, to save herself. His intuition told him that this was a good sign and that now they might have some kind of chance of understanding each other.

Long before he reached her he could hear singing, a strange wordless song. It was wild and lonely and beautiful and he did not at first even remotely associate it with Harriet. When he realised that the voice was coming from somewhere inside the dark foliage of the pear tree his first thought was that the membrane of everyday reality had after all stretched and thinned to transparency overnight, and that like the magical Doors in the Night Maze, the pear tree itself was singing. And there seemed no reason in this new wider world in which he found himself, why a pear tree shouldn't sing to itself ecstatically in the rain.

He stood blinking upwards and saw at last that it was Harriet singing after all. But that seemed hardly less strange. Wrapped in her animal skins like a girl from another time, Harriet sang on oblivious. He thought she had sung herself into a trance.

She sang on for a long while, then the song slowed and ended and she sighed and stretched and laughed softly to herself. He switched on his torch and shone it into the tree, careful not to beam it directly at her.

'Harriet?' he said softly.

Her glasses caught the glitter from the torchlight. Despite his best resolutions he tensed, expecting her to resume her old touchy snapping and snarling at him but she seemed still to be trying to rouse herself from a deep and rather puzzling dream.

'How long have I been up here?' she asked drowsily.

Her oversized furs twinkled with galaxies of caught

raindrops. Her elaborate system of rubber bands had unfastened themselves, liberating a blue-black storm. Framed by this wild cloud her face looked small, vulnerable, grubby and real. Like someone it might after all be possible to make a friend of.

'It's nearly time for supper,' he said.

'Is it still today?' she asked. 'I seem to have forgotten what day it is. As if I've been a long way away.'

'It's still today,' he said. 'You look like a beast in your lair.'

She laughed, moving slightly and knocked down a little avalanche of tiny green pears, hard as pebbles. As he dodged, rubbing his head, she laughed again, but not callously. 'I won't tell you what you look like in that unspeakable anorak,' she said. 'If I must have you for my cousin I shall make Caroline take you out and buy you a new one.'

'I wanted to tell you some things before there was anyone else around,' said Gerard. 'The first thing is sorry. I was wrong not to believe you.'

He waited. There was no point in going on if she wouldn't accept his apology.

'Okay,' she said, rather guardedly, after a long doubtful pause. 'And the second?'

'That's even harder to say,' he said ruefully. 'But Will gave me some things of my mother's and some bits of poetry he'd hidden away in an old shoe box. Basically they were both saying what you told me. Just in different words. Lindsey, my mum, knew about the curse. She was the one Alice chose. Alice is – was – his daughter. The alchemist's daughter. Every generation she chooses someone to help her. But in the end Lindsey was too late. It has to be April, you see. That's when

167

whatever it was happened. And after this year we'll be too old and it will all happen again and again.'

There was no reason why she should listen to him. Listening to himself drivelling on he felt sure she'd think he was trying to make a fool of her. April and alchemy. Poems in shoe boxes. Why didn't he just try to persuade Harriet that it was really perfectly possible to fly away on a pair of wings made out of chicken feathers? He waited in the drizzle, looking down at his mudstained trainers. He couldn't do it alone. He needed Harriet. *She has to choose. She has to choose.*

Harriet, still partly in her green trance, gazed down at him. With a small portion of her mind she still knew the thoughts of falling stars, raindrops and the cells of a pear tree leaf. But the rest of her was an all-too-human fourteen-year-old girl whose bladder was dangerously near to bursting.

'Oh don't mooch around, Gerard,' she said fervently. 'Get me a ladder and help me down.'

And as he turned away to Will's stables in search of a goodsized ladder, she called out, 'I know you mean it, Gerry. I know you do. But oh – do hurry.'

16

The Scheherazade Night

Spending a whole day in a pear tree appeared to have worked some, probably strictly temporary, enchantment on Gerard's cousin. Harriet seemed almost content, at peace with them all, sitting opposite Gerard at the kitchen table, forking up bacon and bubble and squeak and washing it down with mugs of hot tea. Uncle Avery was dining with a client after all. He had telephoned home at the last minute.

Caroline, spooning out healthfood jellies for the twins, was radiant with relief. She didn't even pretend to be angry.

It was funny, thought Gerard. Nothing had changed. Yet everything had. It was true that Harriet still stiffened automatically within Caroline's impulsive embrace when she followed Gerard shyly in through the kitchen, trailing her fur coat like a cast-off skin, wet leaves and blossom caught in her hair. It was also true that she bolted directly to the bathroom and then spent more time there than was strictly necessary, scraping back her hair and skewering it into position. But something had happened to Harriet in the pear tree and because of whatever it was, she and Gerard could now be allies, perhaps even friends. Maybe.

'Let's all go to Leicester tomorrow and do some frivolous shopping and have lunch out,' said Caroline impetuously.

'And buy Gerard a new anorak,' suggested Harriet at once.

Her mother frowned at her.

'Oh it's all right, Mum. I don't think Gerard is emotionally attached to his anorak. I bet he didn't even have that much choice about having it, did you?'

This was an accurate assumption as it happened. There had been a very sticky scene with Norah which it embarrassed him to recall. Besides, he didn't much like being reminded of his poor relation status.

Unexpectedly divining his painfully mixed feelings, Harriet briefly put out her gloved hand towards him. 'I take back my tasteless remark about your anorak,' she said. 'But I warn you, I never grovel. So do you or don't you accept my heartfelt but dignified apology? *Speak!*'

Gerard grinned at once and for an instant their eyes met in a steady exchange of understanding.

'I accept. But I think it's really mean of you to deprive me of a good grovel,' he said at last.

She snorted with surprised laughter which made her tea go down the wrong way rather dramatically and this made them laugh even more.

'Harriet and Gerry are joking to each other,' said Flora, awed, jelly spoon halfway to her mouth, her round eyes widening. She nudged Laurie who was tetchily picking mandarin oranges out of his jelly.

'I'm allergic to these, Mummy,' he grumbled.

'Oh, Laurie, not these little ones, darling. I made it so carefully for you.'

'I *am*,' he said sternly, scratching with an inflamed

170

pink hand at the bright pink patch that was appearing on his forehead. He coughed his sea-lion's barking cough just to prove it. 'I need my inhaler,' he growled, clambering down from the table and off he trudged to find it, barking as he went.

'Meet me in my room,' said Harriet in an undertone. 'But not for too long. I was awake all night. All I really want to do, quite honestly, is sleep for a week.'

Harriet's room was a revelation to Gerard of a hitherto unimagined side to her personality, all swathed Laura Ashley pastel florals, stencilled flowery borders and stripped pine. Not a single waxen image nor a hint of a bat collection in sight.

'Not my choice, I can assure you,' she said noticing Gerard staring round open-mouthed. 'I wanted them to let me have a hammock but they wouldn't. Too sweet for words, isn't it?'

'It is a bit sweet,' he agreed. 'Maybe Flora will like it when she's older.'

'Absolutely sure to, don't you think,' grunted Harriet with a returning flash of her old sourness. She was gloomily unwrapping layers of tissue from something bulky she had taken down from a shelf. 'I just hope she'll like this as well.' She held out a large wooden cuckoo clock and sighed. 'Caroline always wanted one when she was little, you see. So she bought one for me. I hate them. And this.' She brandished a pink velvet-covered jewellery case with a ballet dancer on the top. 'And this.' She indicated a glass snowstorm on her dressing table. 'Caroline never had much of a home. It was all sterile nannies and boarding schools. I think she had a pretty tough time. She tries to give us all the

171

cuckoo clocks and snowstorms she never had.' She shrugged, a thoughtful expression coming into her face. 'I didn't really understand all that before until I just heard myself saying it. But sometimes, Gerry, she makes me feel as if I can't breathe. Parents and children, eh? What a mess. Anyway. Sit down. Find a cushion.'

Gerard was about to retort that she should be so lucky. He was thinking of Errol, his nose pressed to the window of Norah's office every Saturday afternoon. 'Do you think she'll come today, Norah? She'll remember, won't she? Do you think you should phone up? Suppose she's had an accident?'

But then it dawned on him that always being on the receiving end of someone else's misplaced kindness must be as difficult in its way as downright neglect. It left you no freedom to be yourself, to explore the world for yourself. Caroline had too much invested in Harriet's happiness. She couldn't leave anything to chance. Harriet had to have the perfect childhood Caroline never had.

'She's trying to get it right,' he said aloud. 'My mother thought the missing clement was love. So when my father left her, or whatever happened, her whole world fell to pieces.'

Don't cry. It's nothing that can't be mended.

'I'm sorry,' said Harriet awkwardly. 'You've always had to cope with everything all alone. I must seem really spoilt to you.'

'I used to feel really sorry for myself,' he admitted. 'Poor little unwanted orphan.'

He laughed at himself, and sprawled more comfortably on his floral cushion. 'And I still don't think I'd actually recommend it or anything. It doesn't make you

172

feel that wonderful about yourself, but I suppose it left me free to invent myself in a funny sort of way. I mean – '

He looked across at Harriet. He wanted to tell her so much but didn't know where on earth to start.

She was looking at her gloves, picking at them, nervously.

'What's your missing element?' he asked impulsively.

She shook her head silently. She had withdrawn from him into some hidden pain, hunched over, her arms wrapped round herself, rocking slightly, brooding.

He thought: she's better tonight because of being in the tree, but she could still go quite mad one day if we don't put this right. She would just go in and never come out.

'Earth, Fire, Water, Air,' he whispered. 'Met together in a garden fair. Put in a basket bound with skin. If you answer this riddle you'll never begin.'

'Don't. Why did you say that, Gerry? Stop it. It makes me feel all creepy. What is it?'

She had shot bolt upright, putting her hands up to her ears. She looked terrified.

Gerard also felt as if he had unwittingly spoken words of unlocking. For a moment dim listening presences seethed formlessly amongst the shadows, pressing in upon them, closer and closer. He swallowed.

'It's an old riddle. I've heard her sing it – Alice, the alchemist's daughter. Lindsey heard her too. Will said Thomas Noone thought the answer was perfection – *aurum* – does that mean gold? I thought it did. And Alice thought the answer to the same equation was love. Will said they were both right. Do you see? Everybody's

173

trying to get back into Paradise, clutching their little bit of the truth, deaf and blind to everything else.'

Harriet began to say something but Gerard couldn't stop now.

'Look – ' he said, reaching his hand into his pocket, holding out the Gift on his palm. 'This is Lindsey's bit of truth. "You've got to take what you need to survive." That truth was strong enough to lead her away from Owlcote. But it wasn't enough to last her whole life. It didn't lead her to Paradise. It just hurt her in the end. Perhaps it killed her. Harriet, I went into the maze. I know what you think, that it's just a tangle of boring old hedge. But at night it's different. I can't describe it. Everything's in there. I nearly got lost but I had this and I followed it to the doors but I couldn't go any further. *They* told me you had to come. *They* said you had to choose. Everyone in this family has always been alone, Harriet. That's always been the trouble. That's the curse. Everyone on their own, hurting themselves on a little broken bit of the truth. And this is the last chance we'll ever have to change it.'

Listening to his own passionate voice compelling her to believe him, Gerard suddenly had the most extraordinary feeling of expansion, like a paper flower opening out in water. Power flooded through him and with it came a startling new knowledge about himself. It was like finding, no, *remembering*, that he had known all along how to cast spells.

But Harriet was gazing hypnotised at the Gift. 'I can't believe it. So Lindsey took it,' she said at last. 'Granny's ivory bobbin.'

'Is it ivory? I thought it was some kind of bone. Ivory sounds posher. Did you know about it then?'

174

'It was some kind of heirloom. I think it had been in the family since Thomas Noone built this house. My grandfather gave it to Granny. Then one day it vanished. My dad was the last person to touch it. He'd always been fascinated by it. He told Caroline that he had this idea he could take it into the maze and find the what's-it-called. The minotaur. And fight it. So everyone thought he'd taken it for his game and he got into the most terrible trouble. After all, he was his mother's full-time perfect golden-haired boy. Nicking things out of her workbasket wasn't exactly part of the job description. You've seen Granny. You can imagine. And it was wicked Aunt Lindsey all the time. Poor old Dad. I think he still has nightmares about it, though he'd never let on.'

Gerard shivered, remembering the little boy who ran past him sobbing in the maze.

I can't bear it, he thought. I can't bear telling her this. But he knew that in the end he had to and he did. She listened in absolute silence, without once taking her eyes from his face, until he had finished.

Then she said with no expression in her voice: 'A whole tribe of them. In the maze. And every generation the tribe gets a little bit bigger.'

'Yes,' he said grimly.

'And you think – '

'If not you, then Laurie or Flora.'

'Every generation. Unless someone stops it? For ever and ever?'

'Yes.'

It was Harriet's turn to shiver but midway her shivering turned into a compulsive fit of yawning. 'Gerry, I was perfectly serious about there being a family curse but I truly never thought about what it meant. I never seriously thought "Why?" I only thought about how to stop it getting *me*. I never thought about it being mixed up with – oh, awful lonely leftover feelings with a life of their own. It's as though we've all been in prison and don't know it . . .'

She got up to draw the curtains, shutting out the darkness and, still shivering and yawning hugely, wrapped her sprigged quilt around her shoulders. 'Gerry, I'm sorry but I'm so tired I can't think properly any more. My head feels like Caroline's glass paperweight with a snowstorm inside it. I've never needed to sleep more desperately in my life but I don't know if I could now. I don't think I quite want to turn out the light.'

She looked ashamed. 'You'd better not laugh,' she started to say. But another violent yawn wrenched her jaws apart before she could finish her sentence.

'Leave it on, then,' said Gerard. 'Sometimes it used to take a whole packet of Polos before Errol could get to sleep. Only with him it was vampires.'

'You are a comforting soul,' said Harriet, collapsing on to her bed, looking deathly. 'Reminding one of vampires.'

'You need to talk about something really ordinary. If you got properly into bed and covered yourself up so you were comfortable,' said Gerard, 'I could talk to you for a bit if you liked. About really boring ordinary things until you couldn't possibly stand it for a moment longer and simply had to go to sleep to escape my ghastly droning voice.'

She gave her surprised snort. 'All right then, Gerard Noone. *Bore* me to sleep.' She giggled again, slightly hysterically and then hearing it, clamped her hand over her mouth to silence herself. 'You make it sound like Scheherazade in reverse.'

Then she crawled under the bedclothes, took off her spectacles and settled herself into a corpselike pose, assuming an expression of unnerving obedience, like a good child in a film.

And Gerard began to talk, casually enough, lightly, yet somehow always cunningly reaching into himself for the right tone, the right words. Tonight words came to him like birds to a magician's hand, casting spells at his command.

He told her about Norah's Ark and Norah and Phil and how good it had been to find himself cast up at Deben House after all the foster homes. It was almost impossible to believe, he told her, that he had come to be there by accident. Not the fundamentally serious accident of having no parents of his own but a whole series of lesser accidents and benign coincidences that had led him there, step by step, as though by some hidden design.

The Midlands authority responsible for him had decided to give up on foster homes and planned to pack him off to some special boarding school in North Yorkshire. His social worker caught chicken pox and so a young trainee took her place. He was a friend of Norah's. Had actually been, in fact, one of 'Norah's children'. After talking to Gerard on random enjoyable topics like favourite foods, telly programmes, cricket teams, the young man deliberately turned his Citroën 2CV around at the Tadcaster roundabout and drove Gerard all the way back through the Midlands to Deben House in East Anglia where he dumped him, so to speak, in Norah's lap. 'I've seen that school,' Gerard heard him say. 'And it's no place for this kid. It's just the next stop before a remand home, that's what it is. All he'll learn there is breaking and entering and GBH. What's he done to deserve that?'

'It's no place for anyone from what I hear,' said Norah hoarsely, in her smoked kipper Hartlepools. 'Don't worry. We'll keep him here.' And so she did. Gerard never knew how and he didn't care.

'What did she look like?' asked Harriet, her eyes closed. 'I want to imagine her properly.'

'Oh you'd have to see her — she wasn't pretty or anything like your mum. She had a kind of bashed-in look. Battered. With sort of grizzled hair. And she smoked like a chimney. Wonderful example, eh? In a children's home. Oh but she felt safe. She was like a rock. But a warm salty rock, by the sea.'

'One that's stored up a whole day's sun,' said Harriet with intense satisfaction. 'Now tell me about the kids.'

So he told her about gap-toothed Rosalie and Jason, the fantasy game freak, who only ever spoke in what the other kids called Space Burble, a weird improvised language of skreeps and grokes, or in what Phil and Norah called Oracle, a rather high-flown speech mode somewhere between *The Book of Revelations* and *The Return of the Jedi*. Then he moved on to Steven whose enormous ears lit up pink whenever he stood with the lamp behind him and in the end, inevitably enough, he got on to Errol and the birthday present.

'He must have spent hours making it,' he said. 'Colouring sheets of brown paper with smiling balloons. Writing carefully all over it. HAPPY BIRTDAY, it said over and over. Layers and layers of it. And he was standing beside me breathing heavily through his mouth all the time I was unwrapping it. It started off looking like the parcel in pass the parcel. And he was saying over and over like a stuck record, "I know you won't like it. It isn't anything really. It's only ever so small." And when I got right down to the last layer there was this slightly squashed, slightly melted Mars bar.'

'Yuck,' said Harriet. 'Whatever did you say?'

'It's okay. I like Mars bars. I said how had he known to get me such a brilliant present. The best possible present. My favourite thing ever!'

'Did he believe you?'

'Well, I think I may have overdone it a bit. He was searching my face like a radar scanner you see. He was so prepared to be hurt. I couldn't bear it. Then when he saw I was really pleased he couldn't believe it. He grew about a foot taller in front of my eyes. He kept saying, "No one else knew what you really liked, did they?" and "I did that wrapping paper myself, you know." I think it sort of pushed him over into megalomania. He started shoving Bonny and throwing his orange juice around and then he pulled a gargoyle face at Mrs Grist when she told him to behave. I started to get a bit worried then, in case he started imagining he had immortal powers and tried to fly out of upstairs windows or race trains – '

'Oh I want to meet him. Oh poor Errol,' Harriet said. She was up on her elbows, abandoning her good child act, laughing and wiping her eyes. 'Oh dear, Gerry. I feel a bit drunk with tiredness. And if Norah hadn't seen Bee's advertisement, you'd have lived there till you grew up?'

'Yes, I suppose so.'

179

Harriet yawned. He actually heard her jaw crack. Momentarily she closed her eyes. But she still went on talking. 'Don't you hate Granny and everyone? For what happened to Lindsey? And to you?'

'I don't think it's that simple,' he said. 'I used to want someone to blame. As if finding out what or who it was would set me free. Get me back into Paradise, you know. But blaming people is a real dead end. I think that the only way my mum could get away from – the curse, or whatever it is, was to cut herself off from all the rest of you as if you never existed. By a sort of surgery. But if she'd really been free of them she wouldn't have needed to do that, would she? Whatever Will thinks she was still completely connected to them. After my father dumped her, because she was having me, I suppose – actually I think he might have been married. I think that's what she meant about being a thief for love – she went back to her old name. And when I was born she made me into a Noone too. But she was too hurt and proud to go back home for help. She'd landed up in a dead end.'

He was rambling, he realised. He'd just had this dreadful image suddenly of Lindsey trapped in a blind path in the maze: the hedges towering up above her so that it was impossible for her to see how to find her way out.

But there was no response from Harriet. She'd fallen asleep at last, one gloved hand falling loose, dangling towards the floor.

He closed the door softly behind him and went downstairs to tell Caroline not to disturb her. He stayed downstairs for half an hour or so, watching the telly with his aunt. But soon he too was yawning enormously and Caroline packed him off to bed with a hot drink.

Alone in his room again, he went to sit on what he now thought of as Alice's window seat, thinking how queer it was that in trying to comfort Harriet he had accidentally comforted himself.

Not only that, without knowing he was going to do it, he had called forth another hidden self, like a conjurer drawing out shining streamers. A self unlike Lark, distinct from her, yet linked with her. A magician self that gathered fragments of truth together, puzzled over them and played around with them until he thought he could see the pattern that connected them. A self that delighted in turning the fragments into patterns and the patterns into something there had never ever been before. Something round and whole as a robin's egg. Telling stories to Harriet he had found his own way of putting the broken pieces of the universe back together.

Hugging this new secret to himself, Gerard went on sitting for a little longer, drinking his scalding chocolate, looking out over the dark brooding shadow of the maze.

17

Shadow and Light

'Tree therapy,' said Caroline's friend Lottie Pfisterer over the telephone next morning. 'And why should the human spirit not find healing in a tree? Well, *liebchen*, I am happy that your household is now all sweetness, for mine is not. My exhibition is cancelled, Carrie.'

'Oh Lottie, no, I'm so sorry. But there is sure to be another one.'

'No, Caroline. This morning I don't need the tender ministrations of a water snail. Let me just sit in my muddy water and weep. I am angry and frightened and I have a right to be. What I actually need is money. Money to pay my winter heating bill and to buy new silk for my work. And there will be no new exhibition in time to save my bacon.'

'I don't know what to say,' said Caroline.

She waved Flora away and hissed, 'Put your coat on. We're going in a minute.'

'I'm sorry. You were just on your way out. We will talk some other time. But please put your brain to work for me and let me know if you come up with anything. We are not really stupid, are we, Carrie? We are two strong clever women. We have survived worse? Between us we should think of something.'

'Yes,' said Caroline thoughtfully. 'I'm sure we can, Lottie. Try not to worry too much.'

* * *

In the late afternoon, completely dazed with city crowds and traffic, Gerard staggered up the stairs of the Haymarket multi-storey, clutching carrier bags; the stunned owner of a beautiful new jacket, new trainers, two new pairs of cords and four new shirts in complimentary shades.

'You've spent an awful lot on me,' he said anxiously as Caroline, simultaneously carrying Flora across her hip and towing Laurie by the hand peered around in the stale gloom with a baffled expression, and Harriet moaned that Caroline never remembered where she parked the car. 'I hope you can afford it.'

'Oh, Gerry,' said Caroline, stopping in her tracks, oblivious of squealing tyres and the martyred expression of a man in a Volkswagen. She released Laurie's hand and put her arm round Gerard's shoulders. 'I do so hope I haven't offended you or made you feel patronised like a poor relation? Are you sure? I would hate to hurt your feelings. It's just such a pleasure for me to buy you things and, you see, I wish I had been buying things for you for years and years.'

Silently Gerard hoped Uncle Avery would feel the same way. Uncomfortably he remembered that Avery had a Mercedes to keep.

'I want to pop down to the village and talk to Lottie,' said Caroline when they were nearly home. 'I think I might have had a brilliant idea. Shall I drop you two off in the lane so you can run along home by yourselves?'

'Yes,' said Harriet promptly, mouthing at Gerard, '*The maze.*'

He nodded obligingly, his stomach lurching, wondering what secret plans his cousin had been laying for them both. His head still reverberated with traffic noise and the livid lights of changing-rooms. He would quite frankly have preferred a cup of tea and the chance to tune out for an hour or two.

Laurie and Flora had both fallen asleep in their car seats, heads lolling.

Flora's face was tranquil, composed in her sleep, her breath even. But tremors repeatedly crossed Laurie's face as if, like a seisemograph, it registered small storms elsewhere. His cheeks flamed. His mouth quivered, the lips tearfully rehearsing some secret grief or dread. Moaning slightly he flung up a hand, warding off something or someone and within his own body Gerard felt the physical pang of the little boy's fear. The family expedition seemed to have tired Laurie out. But there was nothing sinister in that. Everyone knew little kids tired easily. He closed the door softly behind him and saw that Caroline too turned to look uneasily at Laurie, reaching across the space between them, stroking his hand, saying something Gerard couldn't hear through the glass, before she drove off again with a wave and a bright smile.

Every generation? Unless someone stops it? For ever and ever? – Yes.

Harriet and Gerard set off along the lane in the dazzling April light. A bird zipped over their heads vanishing into a hedge frothy with hawthorne and cow parsley. Everywhere he looked there was blinding bridal white or bursting green but all he could actually see in front of him was Laurie's face, haunted, feverish.

'I don't know if it will be any use,' he said. 'Going in the maze now. In daylight.'

After his earlier feelings of euphoria: behold! a new self with new clothes, he now felt only exhaustion and

184

defeat. The light was too bright, the bird song too piercing, the greens and whites too brilliant, too sharp-edged for the ache in his heart. He would have preferred to see the shadows that were invisibly gathering.

'Well, I think we should test it scientifically,' said Harriet. He realised she was tired and troubled too. Like him she had toiled through overheated, over-crowded chain stores and surged across at traffic lights, all the time inwardly carrying her terrifying truths like a dark brimming bowl that couldn't be allowed to spill over. The shrillness just beneath her voice told him more than her pose of scientific bossiness.

'But your – I mean, Gran said we weren't allowed to go in there. By daylight anyone could see us.'

'Just too bad,' said Harriet, swallowing. The meshed shadows under her eyes stood out against her delicate brown skin like bruises.

She swung herself up over a gate in the hawthorne and headed across the meadow.

'Shortcut,' she said over her shoulder. 'Don't worry,' she added as something snorted and stamped its hooves threateningly behind the hedge. 'They're only bullocks, not bulls. Come on.'

'Right,' said Harriet. 'A quick look round and then run like hell.'

But as they sprinted across the grass in the dazzling light and sharp shadow of the waning afternoon, Harriet moaned aloud with frustration as Will's tall lean figure came loping into view around the side of the house. He hailed them at once and then came pounding up to join them.

'Hallo,' he said cheerfully. 'What are you two con-
spirators up to? Don't look so cross, Harriet. It's
actually Gerard I want to talk to. Carrie tells me you're
a bit of a cricketer.'

'Yes,' said Gerard, interested at once, but uncomfortably aware of the almost metallic clash of rival realities.
'Why?'

Harriet muttered something inaudible.

'Well,' said his uncle. 'The local team is starting up
again after Easter. I thought you might like to try out
for the under-sixteens. That shower usually need all the
help they can get.'

'I'm not a very good fast bowler,' said Gerard. 'Spin
bowling's more my thing. I'm still a bit short, I suppose.'

Will laughed. 'You'll grow. Anyway that was all. You
can gallop off now, Harriet, if you like. Though you
both looked pretty furtive to me. Better watch out the
Krake doesn't look out of the window and catch you.
She reports everything directly back to headquarters.'
He grinned ruefully as if he might have fallen foul of
her once or twice himself. Will worked too hard at
being amiable, Gerard realised, understanding for the
first time why some people were called *disarming*. Will
paraded his boyish harmlessness in the hope that violent
others would put down their swords and cudgels, seeing
he was not worth the effort.

He found himself thinking unkindly: maybe I'll grow
up. But what about you?

'We were just walking down to the river actually,'
said Harriet, coldly. 'I'd like to see anyone make
something out of that.'

But Will, looking at Gerard, was not listening to her.
Pushing his hair out of his eyes he said in a low voice,

186

'It didn't upset you or anything, any of the stuff in that box?'

'No,' said Gerard. For a moment the world shrank down around the man and the boy to an enchanted circle of two. 'Honestly,' he insisted. 'I really didn't understand some of it. But – ' he took a deep breath, 'I would like to know some more about Alice Noone. If there's anything else that you could tell me.' He held Will's gaze steadily. 'She sort of keeps cropping up all over the place.'

For a second or two, Will's gentle face registered something like panic and then he had it almost under control again, except for the momentary biting of his lip. 'Cropping up how, exactly?' he asked lightly but Gerard had felt Will's alarm explode in his own solar plexus. He wants to know if she's spoken to me, but he daren't talk to me about it face to face. For a moment he wanted to shock Will out of his pose of careless indifference, the way he had shaken Harriet the night before by repeating Alice's riddle.

'Well, you know, it's as if she's sort of the house myth. Except that I don't know exactly what the myth is supposed to be. It's so vague, like shapes in smoke. When you reach out, there's nothing to grab hold of. Just feelings.'

Presuming them still to be talking cricket Harriet had wandered away, kicking at grass to vent her feelings.

'House myth,' said Will as if impartially considering something in a book about a fictional family. 'That's a nice phrase.' Then in a different tone he said, hardly audibly, 'Well, every culture has its creation myth and story of the Fall – why not families? Families are kingdoms in miniature after all. Every child secretly

187

knows that. The weak king in the fairy story who lets his daughter suffer is only Dad in disguise and the witch queen – well . . .'

All his assumed cheerfulness was gone now. He seemed to have gone away from Gerard, drifted away into some dreary lightless place inside himself.

'But your grandfather knew things about her,' said Gerard. 'He told them to Lindsey. Perhaps there's someone else somewhere who still remembers being told about it a long time ago. Could you think of someone? An old lady in the village or something.' He found himself unconsciously clutching at Will's sleeve and released it, embarrassed.

But Will just patted him neutrally on the shoulder as if he had already forgotten about him, Gerard thought, or as if he were a tree or a rock. His eyes had dulled. 'It's all too late now,' he said very gently, sweetly. 'Paper aeroplanes, Gerry. Do as I said, make it into paper aeroplanes.'

But you didn't mean it, thought Gerard, wanting to punch his uncle in his frustration at his own inability to come right out with his own truths in the face of Will's nervous evasions. *You wanted me to help. What's changed?*

Harriet came dourly back across the grass, her head down, scowling.

Aloud Gerard said politely, acknowledging defeat, 'Would – would my grandmother like it, do you think, if I went to visit her sometimes? Doesn't she get a bit lonely?'

He had become nervously aware of someone watching them from behind curtains. A face as white as a candle: eyes like holes torn in the air. She was a million miles from the kind of jolly old lady who went in for bridge parties or coach trips to Stately Homes, he thought. For a moment he had a vivid image of her as an old eagle perpetually circling cold barren peaks, half-longing to come down into places of ordinary human warmth, yet dreading and shunning them too.

'Lonely?' Will repeated as if puzzled. 'Well, I never really thought about it, to tell you the truth. She has the Krake for company and so forth. But actually, Gerry, she's not terribly well at the moment. Has trouble with her heart from time to time. So it's probably better to leave her in peace just now. Kind thought though. Extraordinarily kind thought.'

'Oh that's all right,' said Gerard, rather relieved that he wouldn't have to put his kind thoughts into action. 'When she's feeling better then.'

The curtain fell back into place.

Will nodded vaguely. 'That's a good idea,' he said, automatically. He seemed completely withdrawn into himself now so Harriet and Gerard began to trail with a certain understandable reluctance towards the river, looking back. From here, Gerard thought, Will, with his shoulders hunched up around his ears and his hands in his pockets, didn't look much older than Jason at Deben House. Will's inconsistent behaviour drove Gerard nuts but he hated to leave him like this, so bleak and lost. It was as if, under some rough enchantment, he was slowly turning to stone: the human warmth ebbing out of him as the sun sank below the shining rim of the sky.

Harriet seemed to feel the same desire to prove that her uncle was still capable of human response, because she blurted out, suddenly, 'Will, is Bee coming down again soon?'

Even from a distance they saw how Will coloured and then, shifting his feet about, looked awkwardly down at them to avoid looking directly at Harriet and Gerard themselves. He seemed unable to speak for a moment, raising his hands in a helpless gesture as if trying, too late, to intercept something falling. Then he attempted a smile, but seeming to realise that it came out wrong he turned suddenly and walked away.

'She's chucked him then,' said Harriet with the bleak satisfaction of someone whose worst fears are proved right. 'What did I tell you? Oh bloody hellfire and damnation. Now we shall have to walk down to the bloody river.' She set her face in her familiar scowl and stormed ahead, muttering and cursing profanely.

When Gerard caught her up she gave him a cold stare. 'Does my grandmother get lonely sometimes?' she mimicked. 'What a creep. How could you!'

'She's human,' said Gerard. 'Like everyone else. Well, isn't she?'

'I doubt it,' said Harriet savagely. But she seemed too miserable to enjoy a good quarrel.

'It's so silly,' he said, staring out over the budding water iris. 'I like Bee. And Will. And I'm sure they really like each other. So why have they quarrelled?'

Harriet said something inaudible, fiddling with her hairgrips with gloved hands.

'What?' he demanded, suddenly fed up with her self-pity, her endless melodramatic game playing.

'I said, "IT'S THE STUPID BLOODY CURSE!"' she raged. 'And I don't know what to do. It needs someone strong and I'm not strong at all.'

And then, shockingly, Harriet burst loudly into tears.

He led her to a part of the river bank where the grass was short and reasonably dry and sat her down by an elder tree. 'No one's strong,' he said quietly as the sobs came tearing out of her. 'Who's strong, for Heaven's sake? Everyone just does what they can.'

'Norah,' she gulped, when she could get the word out, shuddering with the effort of speech. 'Like a warm salty rock. Remember? Battered old invincible Norah.'

'Not always,' he said. 'She had bad days. On bad days she needed extra nicotine or caffeine or a large slug of whisky in her tea before she could achieve invincibility. I don't think being strong is supposed to be the same as being unshakable – or built like a bomb shelter. It's having the courage to be whatever you are at the time, and keep at it.'

The words came to him out of the wind or from the flowing water. Things he hadn't known he knew. Perhaps he only knew them now. Norah was human. Like everyone sometimes she paid the cost but she had somehow learned to go with the storm. That was the real reason why Deben House was secretly an ark, not a house: not just a children's home.

'But I don't,' she gasped, streaming tears. 'I don't have the courage. Sometimes I'm so scared, Gerry. And there's nowhere to run from it except further and further inside myself. I try to keep it all inside.'

She put her hands up to her face, shielding it from him.

'Why run?' said Gerard. 'Why not just stand your ground and *be* bloody scared?' He was sitting close beside her, almost touching, smiling quizzically when she looked up at him, startled, through her gloved fingers.

To her own evident surprise, she started to laugh then, waterily. 'I don't know,' she admitted. 'I just run.' She began to grope unsuccessfully in various pockets.

'Perhaps, my dear, you have not completely thought this through,' he said, borrowing Phil's mad German psychiatrist's accent. 'Here, have mine. It's fairly clean.'

She blew her nose violently several times but it didn't seem to help much.

'What was good about Norah,' said Gerard, 'was the way she just took everyone absolutely as they were. I always felt she accepted me totally. Warts, weaknesses, wormy bits and all.'

Harriet shook her head. 'I can't imagine it,' she said. 'I can't imagine letting anyone see me without my – my shields.'

'Why?'

She shuddered again. 'I don't know.'

'What would be the worst thing that could happen if they did?'

Norah used to ask that. 'Go on,' she'd say. 'What could be the worst thing that could happen? Well, go out and defy it to happen. Go out and bloody well do it anyway.'

Harriet was silent, looking inward as though inspecting the hideous monster of her self in its reeking pit. 'They'd be disgusted,' she said at last.

'And then?'

'And then I'd, I don't know – die, I suppose. It sounds silly when I say it.'

'So you think you've got to be perfect before you can even come out of your cave and join the rest of the human beings,' he said. 'And as you can't possibly be perfect you think you must be disgusting. But that's awful. It's worse than awful. And your mum and dad are just the same. Can't you see that's part of the curse – that's what keeps the whole stupid tragic thing going. Norah knew enough to love *what's there already* and help it grow. She knew that was the real gold. The real human gold. Not all this "be perfect" garbage. That's fool's gold. False gold. Thomas Noone's curse. Churning out generations of lously lonely alchemists who don't know how to love their lovely brilliant kids because they're kept too busy looking for the one missing element from their own lives. Cinnabar, quicksilver, lapis lazuli, hocus pocus. Must be able to read before you're five, or have long golden hair or be a football ace or a young Einstein or be completely dotty about cuckoo clocks. The thing that's got to be put right before everything can be perfect and – ' He stopped, feeling suddenly tired out with it all. Sick of it.

Harriet was silently picking at her gloves. A large tear came seeping slowly out of the corner of her eye and hung in her lashes. She blinked it away but another at once replaced it. Previous tears had left grubby riverlike furrows down her cheeks.

'I wish,' she said, sniffing hard, 'there was some way people could leave some sort of map around to explain how you are actually supposed to grow up. Oh I don't mean all the details of all the morbid plumbing for making babies and stuff. I mean how do you know – how do you decide you're ready? Does anybody know any more? When's the magic moment? When do you realise you've finally crossed the equator? Because you've got A'Levels? Because you're suddenly old enough to carry on the species? Because you get a driving licence? When does it happen? Do you wake up one morning and suddenly know it – Tarraa! Or do you have to go around just pretending you've grown up when you still feel exactly the same as you always did?'

Gerard grinned and patted her arm. 'I always used to think it must be when you were able to fish out all those squirmy little bits and pieces that get stuck in the plughole, with your bare hand, without cringeing.'

'Oh yes,' said Harriet in squeamish sympathy. 'Or clear up when someone else has been sick.' They both laughed.

'But some people have special ceremonies for it,' said Harriet pursuing her theme. 'To show you aren't a child any more. It's like another kind of birth. You don't have to hang about deciding when you're ready to jump, like someone in a school swimming lesson. There's no chickening out or going back from it. The tribal elders just whisk you off up a mountain on a day of their choosing, or according to the rites or something and leave you there for days and nights until you've met your power animal and dreamed a new name for yourself in a sacred vision. And if you don't get eaten by wolves or fall over a precipice in the dark you come back a certified grown-up and there's no doubt or muddle about it. You can hang it on your wall. Grown up. Done.'

'Harriet Lindany Abdela,' said Gerard, remembering. 'Was that why you used that name? Was that your real name before?'

'No,' she said. 'I don't know what my name was. I don't know what their names were. The archaeologist thing was a story I made up years ago and told myself

194

until it felt true. I found the name in *Ebony* in an article about people trying to reclaim their African identity. I knew what they meant. I knew why. But identity is more than a name or a corn-row hairdo.' She was fidgeting with her plaits, biting her lip.

'A name could be a starting point,' said Gerard.

But Harriet shook her head. 'I was trying to take a shortcut,' she said. 'To being someone else. I was trying not to be like them. Trying to hang on to – I wanted to be – not to be.'

'Not to lose yourself,' said Gerard.

'Yes,' she said. 'I don't want to be spiteful and witchy like Granny Noone but I don't want to be a great soggy blotter for everyone's feelings like Mum either. I want my own life, you see. But I don't know how to – everywhere I look – the choices. It seems so dreadful. As if they've all been used up before I've got to them. All the roads blocked with No Entry or No Through Road. Oh I am sorry, Gerard,' she said, unconvincingly trying to laugh at herself. 'This is like, By the Waters of Babylon I sat down and Wept.'

Sitting with his cousin by the flowing water and the wind-ruffled irises, Gerard wondered how he could tell Harriet of his sudden wild conviction that Harriet's paralysing fear of just about everything was actually, crazily, the key to it all, the key they could use, if only they knew how, to unlock the final door into the past.

'I can't do it alone, you see,' he said aloud. 'I'm not even sure if it's meant for me to do at all. It's you. You have to choose, you know. They told me. With thunder and lightning and everything.'

Again she put up her gloved hands, guarding her face from him. 'I don't know how,' she whispered.

'I don't think you need to know how before you do it,' he said.

He looked back at the lovely old house; Caroline's doves tumbling in the spring light. It looked perfect. From here it was impossible to grasp its inward reality; the pain whirling at its core like a black hole, pulling everything into it, annihilating it. He made up his mind. Now or never.

'We'll go into the maze now,' he said. 'Come on. For your ever so scientific experiment.' He pulled her to her feet. 'Come on, Harriet. No one's around.'

And still sniffing and rubbing a hand across her face, Harriet stumbled after him.

'I suppose I knew it wouldn't work really,' he said, some moments later. 'This is nothing like. It really is as different as night and day. The Night Maze went on forever. This is just like a kid's puzzle; cat's cradle.'

They were at the heart of the maze and he was still ridiculously holding out the Gift which remained dull and inert in the palm of his hand.

'At night it – it was like Doctor Who or something. As if all the old rules of time or space didn't mean anything once you were in here. There was music and voices and visions – a weird kind of procession through time. It was like a dream. But I know it wasn't one, honestly.'

'It's all right. I do believe you,' said Harriet. 'But it doesn't help us much.'

Her voice sounded as if her throat was hurting. She looked around at the straggling box hedges, still sniffing and shivering slightly from crying. A wind was getting up.

Gerard began to drift idly in and out of the arches, scuffing gravel and weeds. 'Earth, Water,' he said softly. 'Fire, Air.'

Why were those words so important? Alice's riddle haunted him. What was the answer Alice longed for as she withdrew further and further from her own time and place: a ghost even in her own lifetime. *Earth, Water, Fire*, he puzzled. He was on the verge of remembering something. Something he had carried inside him always. It was like trying to hook a drowning object out of the water. He just couldn't get near enough.

'Earth, Water, Fire, Air,' he whispered again, touching each arch in turn, wondering if they too lost their true natures in daylight or if it was only human beings who forgot themselves and were deceived by appearances, losing themselves in mazes they themselves had made.

Harriet watched him silently. Behind her spectacles, her eyes were elusive again, masking her fear.

'If each of these was a door into another world, a world like a totally new planet, like that hymn about the blackbird and the first morning – which would you choose?' said Gerard, dreamily, his head still stuffed with light, unearthly music, distant thunder.

'I don't know,' said Harriet, rather too quickly. 'I haven't thought about it.'

'You're allowed to think about it.'

'But I don't want to.'

Her face was ashy, her eyes veering away from him as if she feared a trap. He began to walk away from her, giving the whole thing up as beyond him for now, singing the words which rang more and more loudly in his head.

' – met together in a garden fair. Put in a basket bound with skin. If you answer this riddle you'll never be – '

But what *happened*, he puzzled. What happened to Alice Noone in the cruellest month when everything was green and blossoming and bursting with birdsong?

Afterwards he thought he must have felt Harriet call him rather than heard her. He was sure she made no sound yet someone's terror shrieked in his head, high frequency, and he swung round in a stinging shower of gravel to find her crumpled to her knees, her eyes fixed in horror upon the empty space between the arches.

'You called her,' she whispered, staring, appalled. 'You called her and she came.'

'But I only turned round for a minute,' he protested. 'There wasn't time.'

'I saw her,' she insisted numbly. 'You called her. She looked as if she wanted to answer you but she was too far away somehow. It was as if she'd been sort of emptied out and there was nothing left but fear. *I saw her, Gerard.*'

'We should go,' he said. 'We ought to go.'

He didn't like what had happened to Harriet's face. It had gone all stiff and staring.

'Come on – we'll go now,' Gerard said again urgently, putting his hand on her shoulder.

Myths are supposed to stay underground, he thought. People can't bear the power of it when they meet them face to face. Stuff safely tucked away in books and poetry is one thing. But ghosts in Supersave, monsters in the multi-storey, that's something else. That's why

198

you have to look in the shield when you meet Medusa. That's why they made the maze forbidden. So nobody has to face it head on and risk going out of their heads with the horror of it.

Harriet didn't move. 'I saw her before,' she said, through her stiffened lips. 'I saw her when I was in the tree. But it was safe in the tree because I felt part of everything, you see. Not alone like a broken bit of something else like I usually do. So the hurt and the sadness was part of everything else, like some sort of almost peaceful kind of pattern – I don't know – light and shadow. Flowing in and out of each other. But here all I could feel was the awfulness, as if you could fall into it like a hole in the world and get swallowed up forever. Oh, Gerard.'

Her breath began to come in great rapid wheezing gasps. She snatched off her glasses as though that would make it easier to deny what she'd seen. Her eyes blazed at him, enormous. Naked, her stricken face was a featureless blur from which all other colour had drained.

'Her hair hung in her eyes, like a mad person's, as if she didn't even notice it any more. Something crawled out of it. There were sores round her mouth, and on her legs.'

She pressed a gloved hand against her mouth for a moment, swallowing with difficulty, as though she was afraid she was going to be sick. 'She was a real person, Gerard, and he let her suffer. His own daughter. She was so thin – all her bones were sticking out. Like a child in a famine. She was like someone who has slowly been forgetting day after day after day, how to be human. All she wanted was for him to love her, but he

199

couldn't.' Her voice failed in her throat, becoming a thinned-out wail.

'She wanted you to see her,' said Gerard. 'I think I saw her in the maze. She was stroking a wild half-grown fox in the snow and she looked wilder than the cub.'

Harriet was suddenly on her feet, trembling. 'I want to go back,' she said. 'I've got to go back. This is too real. I can't bear it.' And turning, blindly, she bolted from the maze. As he hurried after her, he could hear her blundering ahead of him, gasping for breath between almost soundless sobs, and once he heard her moan in a low frantic voice: 'I can't do it. I can't do it. It's no use.'

She sat bolt upright in the dark. Her hair was soaked with perspiration. I didn't dream, Harriet told herself. I never dream. But her heart was racing, her mouth parched with fear.

There had been a clear sky streaming light. People in unfamiliar clothes were playing music, dancing and laughing around the house, out in the gardens. They were people she had known for always.

Then a pale child sitting by herself in the window, apart from everyone, pointed at a speck in the sky that grew nearer and larger even as they watched, borne upon a thrumming droning sound as though upon a mighty wind, and as it grew nearer still it became denser, heavier, darker as like some deadly sponge it began to absorb into itself all the light. Like a shrill wild bird the child screamed, 'The owl!'

And the light and life in the house drained away, all sucked into the nightmare being that overspread the

200

house with leaden wings. Now the darkness thickened like pitch. Everything was silent except for the terrible thrumming of its wings. Then as the air was torn from her lungs, Harriet screamed like Alice, 'The owl! The owl!' And woke half-suffocated in stifling darkness and for a terrible moment, no longer knew if she was Alice or Lindsey or herself, Harriet.

But even as she began to calm herself she heard Laurie screaming on the floor below and knew his terror was identical to the terror that had wakened her seconds before. Before she had time to think she found herself at the foot of her staircase, on the landing outside the twins' room. Caroline was hurrying from her own room, calling comfortingly so that Laurie should know help was coming.

'Make it stop! Mummy, make it stop – I can't – I can't – *Mummy!*'

The little boy was choking, struggling for air, scarlet.

Flora stumbled blearily across the space between the beds, clutching Laurie's inhaler. 'I've got it, Mummy,' she yawned. 'I'm sorry. My legs wouldn't work properly.'

'I can't – I can't – Make it stop,' gasped Laurie, his eyes staring wildly around as though he was still trapped in his nightmare. His chest laboured for air and he was frantically pushing away something invisible. 'Don't take the light, Mummy. Don't let – Don't – '

'Laurie, Laurie. I'm here, darling. Of course no one will take your light. Look. I've switched it on. It's still here, sweetheart. Your very own little light.' She snapped a switch and a toadstool-shaped lamp floated at once upon the eucalyptus-smelling darkness.

Still heaving with great rasping breaths, Laurie looked

dazedly round at the familiar shadows of his night time room. Slowly he recognised Flora standing yawning in her pink nightie and Caroline sitting quietly beside him on his bed.

Finally he took in the perplexing presence of Harriet who had come uncertainly to the other side of his small pine bed and now stood dishevelled, scattering hairpins, shivering slightly in her crumpled striped pyjamas. Then bursting into noisy tears he launched himself at his big sister, hurling himself inside the safety of her arms, sobbing, 'It was the owl, Hatty. It was the owl. It was the horrible owl again. Don't let it come. Oh Hatty. Don't let it come again.'

And just as she had come down a flight of stairs without knowing it, Harriet mysteriously found herself rocking her little brother in her arms, his damp curls against her cheek, muttering fiercely over and over, 'It won't come. It won't get you, Laurie. It's all right. It will all be all right. I promise you. I'll look after you.'

18

Flesh and Blood

When Gerard went into Harriet's room next morning he was greeted by an angry whizzing sound and the sweet parched smell of drying newly washed hair.

'Damn,' said Harriet, looking up and seeing him, talking through the combed hair she was carefully holding between her teeth, while the hand that wasn't wielding the drier raked and tugged at a recalcitrant black cloud. 'I hate people watching me do my hair. Couldn't you at least have knocked?'

'I did,' he said, just for the form of it since she didn't seem as angry as she was pretending or as loony as he had dreaded. 'You didn't hear because of the drier. Are you okay? You were a bit – '

'I was pathetic,' she said briefly. 'You needn't be so polite. If I'd have been you I'd have kicked me. Listen, Gerry. Whatever it is we've got to do – ' She stopped worrying away at her tangled hair, spat out the combed strands, pulled it all roughly into a band and simply left it to wander loose all down her back like a small black storm. Then she came over to sit beside him and made a shrugging open-handed gesture as if to say, where do we go from here?

'You look awfully tired,' he said.

'Laurie was really ill in the night. Caroline's taken him to the doctor. She's awfully worried about him but not as worried as I feel, Gerry. He went off into a full-blown asthma attack. He had his nightmare. You know, the family one. The one we all busily pretend we don't have. I had it too. When I woke up I didn't know who I was, or *when* I was. I think for a moment I was Alice and Lindsey as well as me.'

He pushed Will's exercise book at her, folded back at the last page. As Harriet studied the bad drawing silently, her face became tense and mask-like. She stared and stared at the child with its starfish toes, its scribbled nightdress, the lopsided bottle in its hand, standing between the elaborately crayoned doors at the centre of the maze.

'Lindsey did it,' he said. 'When she was still quite small I'd guess. When she could still understand Alice properly. Before things got in the way. I looked at it this morning before I was properly awake and suddenly I realised I was looking at a scene straight out of one of my own dreams. One I must have had all my life but never managed to remember. Perhaps I inherited it from Lindsey, if you can inherit dreams. In it I am running and running down endless dark paths, twisting and doubling back on themselves like snakes. They seem to have a horrible life of their own. And the whole place is soaked in fear. And I'm shouting 'Don't!' because I've got to stop some terrible catastrophe but I know I never can. And I can hear her singing her sad creepy song – '

'Gerard!' Harriet was gripping him painfully by the arm as if she wanted him to stop before it was too late.

'And then just as I reach her, she's unstoppering this bottle and putting back her head – '

'Don't,' whispered Harriet, her lips dry, her eyes burning, as if she was watching him unfasten the final catch that would release all the wars, plagues and famines of the world from its box of darkness.

'And she starts to drink – I've been calling out to her but I can't get close enough to touch her and I keep thinking if only I – '

Harriet sat up straight. He heard her take a sharp inward breath. Forcing herself, she began to speak, overlapping with his own words like the next singer in a round.

'And she starts to change. From the soles of her feet all the way up her body. And then a man bursts out of the darkness with a burning torch in his hand and she turns and she cries out in this hoarse inhuman voice, "Now will you love me?" And then I turn and run and run to get away from the sight of her turned to gold and the sound of *him* sobbing and shouting.'

They were staring stricken at each other. Unconsciously they reached out, grasping each other's hands.

'That was the last door,' said Gerard. 'You didn't hold it shut. You helped me open it. You were frightened. But it didn't stop you.'

'Everything feels so weird.' Harriet swallowed, looking around her warily. 'And everything looks different. The same but different.' She laughed shakily.

To Gerard too there was some subtle alteration in the air or light as though the alchemist's house was listening to them. Listening and waiting.

'She poisoned herself, didn't she?' he said. 'She watched and waited until she somehow got hold of the key to his secret room, his laboratory, and when he was out of the house she crept in and found a bottle of whatever it was – his precious elixir for turning junk to

205

gold and then she took it off with her into the maze so that it would be too late before anyone found her.'

'And it was – he was too late,' said Harriet. 'He must have known underneath all the time what he was doing to her but he couldn't allow himself to feel what it was like for her. He was so angry at losing everyone he loved, so angry that his Elizabethan paradise had been destroyed, that it wasn't perfect any more, that he couldn't let himself feel even a spark of love for Alice, couldn't let her help him.'

'He thought it was weakness to need help,' said Gerard. 'He wasn't any kind of grown-up when it came to it. He wasn't a father. He was a super-clever big kid in disguise and when the world stopped being his sunny playground he fell apart. He shut all his grief and horror up inside himself and went dashing off, mad as a hatter, kidding himself he was on a Great Mission. Maybe he thought: when I've finally unlocked this great cosmic secret, maybe shared the wisdom of all the heavenly angels, made a few notes, then I'll have time to notice her, pity her. And all the time she was living in his house, fading, getting ghostlier and ghostlier.'

'Gerard, the house is listening,' said Harriet, echoing his own earlier thought.

'I feel as if it's speaking through me with angry voices,' he said.

'Angry and sad,' she said, getting something out of her eye.

Because it was breakfast time they went downstairs to find some food, but both felt too quiet and strange to eat much. While they were still clearing up, Caroline came in with the twins. Laurie, still audibly wheezy, was waving a fancy inhaler.

206

'Look,' he said, beaming. 'This one's going to make me better.'

'Good,' said Gerard, stacking dishes. 'I'm glad to hear it. It's very boring being ill, isn't it?'

Laurie laughed like an old accordion, leaning up against Harriet who moved him gently out of her way and then tickled his cheek. 'I'm a bit used to it now,' he confessed.

Caroline looked exhausted. 'Oh, is there some coffee left?' she said. 'You angels.'

Harriet poured her out a mugful.

'So what does Lottie think of your plan?' asked Gerard. 'You never got around to telling us what it was yesterday.'

'Oh that,' said his aunt miming total collapse. 'I can't imagine how I ever had the energy to think of that! She thought it was wonderful as it happens. I suggested we could combine our talents and do a bit of small-scale catering. Lottie really fizzes away like a sparkler when something fires her imagination. When I left she was tearing through the phone book, looking for potential customers, and people who'd let us have wholesale broccoli and wild rice and I don't know what.'

Flora growled experimentally to herself. 'Wild rice, Mummy,' she said, laughing. 'Listen.'

Suddenly Caroline's expression became a little fixed.

'What's up?' said Harriet at once. 'Why are you staring? Spot on my nose?'

'No – no of course not, darling. I was just thinking – your hair. It's very nice.'

Harriet put up her gloved hand to the back of her head, acutely suspicious. 'Ow – oh bloody hell!' she exclaimed and bolted from the room.

'Oh dear,' said Caroline. 'And it did look so nice. She looked so sweet, Gerard.'

'But Harriet thinks being sweet is feeble,' Gerard pointed out. 'Fragile people are sweet. The kind of people who can be got at by other people. She'd much rather be sour.'

Caroline laughed aloud at this.

'When she was up in the pear tree,' he said, 'she was singing. Really singing, but without words. It was nice. Peculiar but very nice.'

'She used to do that when she was small. Almost as soon as she could talk – no, before. She used to lie in her cot carolling away. Sometimes songs I'd taught her but mostly it was songs of her own. Songs without words. Until she went to school. She didn't do it any more after she went to school.'

Caroline sighed, passing her hand over her face, but to Gerard's relief, before she even had the chance to start running herself down again, the phone rang and she had to go and answer it.

'That was Lottie,' she said, when she returned. She looked slightly appalled but amused despite herself. 'She's got us our first job already. After the Easter holiday! I thought we'd start out gently, you know, testing the local market, feeling our way: *vol-au-vents* and frozen Black Forest gateau for the local Masonic Ladies Night or something suitably low-key. But not Lottie. She's booked us to do cordon bleu for forty: home-made pâté and I don't know what. I said, "Whatever sort of pâté, Lottie," and she said, "Chicken liver, *liebchen*. I know a man who runs a free-range farm and he's letting us have fifteen pounds tonight. I've told him to deliver them to your place. My kitchen is far too small." '

'Fifteen pounds?' asked Gerard. 'Won't that make an awful lot?'

'About enough to stock an entire supermarket chain, I should think,' said Caroline. 'We'll be up all night.'

She began to laugh. 'Well, thank Heaven Avery has to stay in Lincoln tonight. With any luck we'll have it under control by the time he comes back.'

It occurred to Gerard that Caroline had not told Avery about her plan for rescuing her friend from the clutches of the bailiffs. But before he could pursue this thought Harriet appeared again, her hair rebraided, her expression defying comment. Yet something was different. Gerard couldn't exactly make out what it was because he wasn't very well up on girls' hair and what they did to it. But it seemed to him that her forehead bulged a little less than before. This morning, he thought, she doesn't look quite so much like a bolting horse.

'We'll help,' he said aloud. 'We'll help, won't we, Harriet?' he appealed to his cousin.

'Help with what?' Her tone implied that her help was most unlikely whatever it was.

'Help me, your mother. Deal with a secret consignment of chicken livers before your father gets home,' said Caroline cryptically as she left the kitchen.

Harriet frowned. 'Did I miss something vital?'

'I'll tell you as we go,' said Gerard.

For the next few hours of Gerard and Harriet's day, on the surface, everything was quiet and uneventful. But somewhere, just out of vision, Harriet sensed the grieving Alice flickering in and out of her own time like a faulty light bulb. Sometimes Gerard caught snatches of meaningless whispering in passageways or muffled weeping on the stairs.

Sitting around the solid table in the warm present-day kitchen, his feet firmly on the tiled floor, Gerard wished he could not simultaneously feel Alice pressing herself against the walls, willing her body of human flesh and bone and blood to dissolve into its separate elements, allowing her to pass at last like a spirit of fire or air, through the solid stone. She had reached the limit of her pain, he thought. The cruellest day of the cruellest month.

Once Harriet said abruptly to him in an undertone when they were supposed to be playing a quiet game with the twins, 'She's got the key to his room. His secret room. She'll use it tonight.' And then a shadow of puzzlement crossed her face as if she had just heard what she said. Since the dream-sharing experience, as if Harriet had truly permitted the door of the past to be unlocked, Alice was more intrusive, more insistent than ever, yet still heading inexorably, it seemed, for the same stark fate.

Before coming to Owlcote, Gerard had always thought of time as something similar to distance. The longer ago something was, the farther it was from you. But now he knew better. If there was some powerful connection between them, people living in different times could reach out across centuries and touch each other unknowingly with their thoughts.

She's got the key, he thought. *How can we stop it happening again? How can we possibly?* Laurie

210

coughed patiently into his mansized tissue. Harriet threw the dice again and reminded Flora to move her counters the right number of spaces. And on and on the dark disturbing river ran.

Lottie breezed in, after supper, tiny and vivacious in jeans and a stylish silk shirt, her eyelids grass green, her silvery blonde curls expensively cut; scarcely the image of someone on the breadline in Gerard's stern view. But, Harriet whispered, Lottie would somehow contrive to dine on avocado and wear silk whatever else she went without. It was just that she had certain standards she didn't care to let slip. Laughing and gesturing, talking a blue streak, as she comically enveloped herself in a drowning apron, Lottie, though tired herself, enlivened and invigorated everyone so that the enforced pâte-making session now seemed as if it had already turned into a party. But having once begun, it went on, as Caroline had known it would, and on and on for hours.

'I was worrying about what I might dream again tonight,' hissed Harriet in Gerard's ear. 'But now I know — flaming chicken livers!' She went back to crushing juniper berries between sheets of greaseproof paper, averting her face and shuddering at the smell which she said was like something rotting in a hedge.

Lottie and Caroline were both tired to begin with and what with their physical exhaustion, the lateness of the hour and the rapid depletion of the enormous bottle of wine Lottie brought with her, they soon became hilarious.

Laurie had come downstairs again, 'feeling wheezy,' as he said: wrapped in his fleecy dressing-gown and settled cosily in a chair beside the Aga, his eyes wide with astonishment at his mother's increasingly cheerful behaviour.

'*Liebling*,' Lottie called across the kitchen from where she was briskly preparing several earthenware dishes for the finished product. 'Are you quite sure you have never in your career played in *Macbeth*?'

Caroline looked puzzled for a moment and then began to laugh throatily with comprehension, looking at her fingers, now bloodied from scooping handfuls of minced livers into the china mixing bowl. 'What – will these hands ne'er be clean,' she cried, flourishing scarlet hands.

She and Lottie began to hoot like a pair of dim-witted schoolgirls, collapsing into the nearest chairs, almost weeping with laughter at the farcical situation they had created for themselves.

At that moment the door from the hallway opened and Uncle Avery strolled into the kitchen obliviously unfastening his cuff-links, then froze, appalled.

There was a stricken silence.

Then Lottie and Caroline's eyes met, flickered involuntarily across the room to Avery's scandalised expression and they began howling with laughter all over again. When at last Caroline was able to speak, she gestured towards her husband and babbled, 'Fye my lord, fye! A soldier and afeard.'

'What is the meaning of all this,' said Avery rigid with disapproval.

'Poor old Avery – he's always turning up in the wrong play,' said Caroline compassionately.

'Avery, we confess! You have caught us red-handed,' cried Lottie.

212

At which Harriet, whose face had become a mask of tension, giggled. Infected by the high wild sound, Gerard began to grin too and Caroline and Lottie, utterly beyond redemption now, went off into helpless hysteria.

Laurie, looking helplessly from his almost unrecognisable cackling bloodstained mother to his dangerously white silent father, began to look frightened. 'Mummy,' he pleaded. But no one heard.

'I suppose there's some perfectly reasonable explanation for turning a family kitchen into a slaughterhouse,' said Avery.

Caroline, with a valiant effort, straightened her face. 'We thought you were going to be in Lincoln till tomorrow,' she said.

'Is that supposed to be some kind of logical reply?'

'Maybe not logical,' admitted Caroline, 'but true.' Her eyes darkened.

'Avery, Carrie was helping me,' said Lottie, who had also sobered down. 'I needed to make money in a hurry and she had the idea that together we could cook for people, for buffets and so on. And this was our first attempt.'

'And it didn't occur to you to ask me first,' said Avery to his wife as if only the two of them were present.

'No,' she said. 'Because I knew you wouldn't like it.'

She was over by the sink now, running her bloody hands under the taps. Lottie hurriedly gathered up the enormous bowl of minced livers, looking around wildly as if she hoped she might be able to hide it somewhere.

Caroline dried her hands, visibly trembling now.

'You mean that I didn't ask your permission. That's what you mean,' she said. She wouldn't look at him but

213

began agitatedly gathering the remaining ingredients so she could help Lottie mix them together. 'The mace,' she said in an undertone. 'We've forgotten the mace and allspice.'

'I'll get it,' said Lottie, almost whispering.

It was as if someone had died. Gerard was finding it hard to breathe. He kept remembering how frightened Harriet had been when she dared to speak her nightmare aloud. Between them they had prised open a box of darkness that the Noones had kept buried for centuries. And now the air was full of flying malevolence, sharp-edged as razors. *Something terrible is going to happen.*

'Stop it!' Avery bellowed so suddenly that Laurie jumped physically with fright. 'What is this – a coven? You two mumbling away to each other like a pair of witches! I'm still here, you know, Caroline, and I'm trying to talk to you.'

'You are not talking to me, Avery,' said Caroline, still not looking at him, mixing the ingredients with great gory scoops of her wooden spoon. 'You are shouting at me and trying to browbeat me like you always do. And I've had enough. So stop being so pompous and melodramatic and make yourself a cup of tea and sit down like an ordinary human being – or even *help us*, for God's sake, what about that for an eccentric idea? And then we can all clear up this awful bloody mess and get to bed.'

'Mummy,' said Laurie, catching his breath. But he was overtaken by a fit of coughing and no one heard him.

Avery had just spotted the almost empty wine bottle.

'You've been drinking!' he said accusingly. 'You're both drunk. My God.'

'Don't be so ridiculous,' said Caroline, her wonderful voice cracking out like a fiery whip. 'I refuse to let you control me – therefore I must be drunk. And that *is* logical, is it?'

'Caroline, Laurie's ill,' said Gerard urgently.

The little boy was turning blue, fighting for breath. Caroline was across the kitchen in two strides.

'Harriet, get his inhaler,' she ordered. 'Hurry! It's by his bed.'

'Mu – Mummy – I can't – ' gasped Laurie.

'Don't try to talk, darling. Don't panic, sweetie. Look, remember what we do. Slow, slow breaths like this. In . . . out . . .'

'Here it is.' Harriet hurtled back into the kitchen and Caroline seized the inhaler.

'Come on, Laurie, did we frighten you? You mustn't worry. It was just a silly quarrel like the ones you have all the time with Flora. Come on, slow breaths. In and out . . .'

Avery was whiter than wax. He gripped the back of the kitchen chair as if it was the only thing keeping him on his feet. 'This is your fault,' he said. 'You and your stupid – '

'Shut up, Avery,' said Lottie. 'Tell us later how stupid we are. At the moment we don't have time to listen. Let me do something, Carrie. A warm drink?'

'No, Lottie. I think I'd better phone ahead to the hospital and tell them I'm bringing him in. Can you sit here with him just for a minute? Harriet, grab his coat and the travel rug. He'll need to be wrapped up because the heater's on the blink. Sweetie, shan't be a minute, don't cry. I'll get you very quickly to the hospital and you can have a little whiff of oxygen and then you'll feel wonderful again.'

But by now Laurie was completely blue. He was far too terrified to listen to anyone. His hands flailed in the air, feebly struggling with something invisible. It looked as if he was slowly drowning before their eyes.

Avery still stood clutching the chairback, paralysed. Then as Caroline came back into the kitchen, her car keys in her hand and her coat half on, he made a sudden scrabbling dive for the back door. 'I've got to go back to the office,' he barked, his voice authoritative, but looking desperate. 'I've forgotten to lock something up.'

And he bolted out into the darkness.

'My God,' said Lottie. 'I don't believe it.'

But Caroline's thoughts were all for the children. 'Lottie, please could you take Flora home with you for tonight? If these two need anything, Will can keep an eye on them. I'll phone from the hospital. Come on, darling,' she said, bundling Laurie up in the tartan rug. 'I've got you safe. Just a little trip in the car. Quite an adventure. Just you and me, that's it. Off we go.'

And she was gone.

Minutes later Harriet and Gerard saw Lottie off to her car with a wide-eyed Flora in her arms, peering around in drowsy puzzlement at the starry spaces that had replaced her bedroom ceiling.

Then they were left alone to confront the macabre remains of the evening's work.

'I do hope he'll be all right,' said Gerard, feeling wretched.

Harriet nodded, not trusting herself to speak.

216

'Did we make that happen?' he said. 'I feel as if we made it happen.'

Before it had been underneath, locked in like a swollen underground river. Now, Gerard thought, it had finally smashed its way out and come bursting upward, knocking them all off their feet, dragging them where it would in the fury of release.

'What should we do with all this, do you think?' he asked, looking around the gore-splattered kitchen with depression.

Alice has unlocked the door. She is taking down the bottle.

But the horrific present claimed all that remained of their flagging energies.

Harriet, who had fallen into a chair, staggered to her feet again, looking like death. 'We'd better clean it all up,' she muttered.

'We could put this bowl of liver stuff in the fridge,' he suggested. 'Then they can cook it tomorrow if – if everything's okay by then. So all we really have to do is wash up and sluice all the work tops down.'

Harriet managed a grim smile. 'Lottie always says that she cooks like a hurricane,' she said. 'But this looks more like a massacre to me.' Her grin faded. 'Bad joke,' she muttered. 'Bad joke.'

When they were almost halfway through cleaning up the phone rang and Harriet tore off to answer it.

'It was just Bee,' she said when she trailed back. 'She wanted Caroline. She sounded as if she'd been crying. I told her what happened and she said she'd ring tomorrow to find out how he is.'

Picking up her cloth, she wrung it out in the plastic bucket and went back to work.

By the time they had finished and made themselves a desperately needed hot drink, it was after midnight and still Avery had not returned.

'Shouldn't you phone his office?' asked Gerard.

She shook her head. 'What can he do? You saw him . . .' But she didn't say whatever she had been going to say. Gerard wondered if she was angry with Avery or just resigned, or if like him she had been wrung with a terrible pity to see her father glued to the chairback, white and silent: incapable of taking one step towards his own small son to help or comfort him.

'He had to go to hospital before with his asthma,' said Harriet. 'When he was about eighteen months old. He was in for weeks. Caroline plays it down but I think he nearly died.' She looked steadily back at Gerard and he recognised something new in her expression. He had seen it earlier, he realised, when she wrung the bloody water heedlessly from her cloth.

Then she went silently out into the hall. When she came back she was putting on her jacket.

'I promised him I'd keep him safe,' she said. 'I promised I wouldn't let the owl get him.'

Gerard gaped at her. Sometimes people could knock you for six. He thought of her weeping on the river bank, and bolting from the vision of Alice in the maze. He could see she was trembling. She just stood there, shaking in her shoes but looking determined.

She held out her hand. 'Can you bear to lend it to me? I think I'm supposed to use it.'

He groped in his pocket. 'I'll come with you,' he said.

'No,' she said. 'Though I'd love you to. You can come later but not now. You know what tribal elders are like. It's up the mountain on your own, mate, or else no blooming certificate.' She managed a smile.

He held out his hand to her, the Gift balanced on the palm.

'You can look up,' he said huskily. 'It helps a bit.'

She took it from him awkwardly and stood at a loss, suddenly, clutching it in her gloved hands. 'Last chance for the Noones,' she said simply at last. 'Last chance, eh?'

Then with a straight back, her face fierce and terrified, she strode past him and out of the kitchen door.

And Gerard, finding she hadn't quite closed the door after her, watched the lonely figure in its light waterproof jacket, bobbing away into the country darkness, growing smaller and smaller until his straining eyes could no longer distinguish her. But just before he closed the door it seemed to him, that he caught a glimpse of something else, nothing much to go on, like a moth-like flicker of white out of the corner of his eye, no more. But he knew it was her, Alice, the alchemist's daughter.

19

Golden Touch

Harriet stood alone at the entrance to the maze.

She was sick and shaking. Inside her gloves, her hands were clenched fists. Perhaps Laurie was dying in the hospital. And if he didn't die this time, if he lived until he was eighty, he would live a half-life, the half-life of all the Noones. She forced herself to face it. Avery, apparently invincible in his study among his law books, was lost, huffy and infantile in the kitchen. While Caroline, her mother, could never stop pouring love and tenderness into her family for one moment because if she did she would have to recognise that it simply wasn't possible for one person to love enough for two parents; Caroline's love was really for the needy child she herself had been, the needy child she still was, terrified that her longed-for family would vanish like a mirage if she failed them even once.

For the first time Harriet understood that, in her headlong flight from the confusions and betrayals of her family, she had somehow become trapped behind elaborate defences meant to keep her safe. But the twins had no such defences against Caroline and Avery. Like seedlings that had shot up too far in a lopsided light they were brilliant and precocious in some things, but sickly and blighted in others.

She took a blundering half step into the darkness.

I'm afraid. I'm not ready.

It's like another birth, she had told Gerard, rashly. Her big mouth. There's no going back. When the tribal elders send for you, that's it.

Why did I want that? Why couldn't I just be content with being half-awake, watching other people live at second-hand on the telly.

She took a second step.

I live in different times. If I want elders I shall have to whistle them up myself. Divide myself up; old wise woman and young scared girl. Call for myself in the night and answer. Send myself up the mountain. *I have to guide myself.*

A third step. She gasped.

She hadn't realised such cautious steps could take her so far, for totally unprepared and quite without meaning to she had crossed over some invisible threshold. At one stroke, the sounds of the night garden were wiped out. She was inside the Night Maze. Darkness gathered her in.

She was lost, drowning in darkness. The silence hurt her ears. Laurie's terrified face floated before her. She had promised him. She loved him, she discovered. She would do anything to save him. But she knew she could be no use to him until she first saved herself. That was what Caroline didn't understand. You couldn't skip out the stage of saving yourself and do it second-hand through other people.

She was still too afraid and disorientated to move. Suppose she was stuck there forever, like Lot's wife; her fear crystalised around her in a glittering white rind. A girl of salt. A girl of flesh and blood. A girl of gold. *Which am I?* The words drummed in her mind as though someone chanted a ritual incantation. Somewhere an old woman, practically toothless, chanted tunelessly; monotonously drummed, her brown hands a rapid blur on the stretched hide, summoning her further into the dark.

You can look up, Gerard had said. But what if it was a cloudy night? Doubtfully she raised her head.

Just look at them! She felt as if she had never really looked at stars before. Pulsing and burning with their ancient fire as if they had some kind of message for her.

I have to choose. I have to choose a door.

But the choice, she understood, had already been made long ago by some older part of herself. It was accepting the choice, that was the hard, no, the impossible thing. She wouldn't think about it. Not yet.

The Door of Fire, she thought. I'll concentrate on finding it first and not on what I might have to do when I get there.

She put her hand into her pocket and brought out the Gift, holding it on her palm in front of her in imitation of Gerard's strangely open gesture. But it remained inert and invisible in the darkness. Nothing happened.

It doesn't work for me, she thought in terror. *Oh God, I might have known!*

Imploringly she lifted her eyes again to the fiery tracks of the constellations.

Another maze. A maze of light and I'm stuck down here in the dark. It's a pity we can't get together.

Then she understood. Gerard had held the Gift in his bare hand. If Harriet wanted the Gift to guide her she would have to take off her glove. Fear flashed through her from the soles of her feet to the crown of her head. *I can't – it's too dangerous. Everything I touch . . .*

222

She was cursed. Her family had cursed her. Life itself had cursed her. All her gifts would always turn upon her like knives in the air. But somewhere behind the panicky voices in her head was another tentative voice asking might it be possible, could a person – change a curse back into a gift?

She had to try. For her own sake and for Laurie. For Caroline and Avery. She must touch the bobbin with her naked hand. She must take the risk. If she didn't it would all happen again and again.

'Oh how I hate this,' she moaned aloud, her teeth chattering as she peeled off her right glove. 'I can't destroy it. I can't curse it. This is the right thing for me to do.'

Please let that be true.

Shaking so violently that her breath could only escape in explosive gasps and shudders, Harriet transferred the Gift from her gloved hand to her naked right hand.

Her eyes widened.

First the bobbin quivered and shifted like a compass needle, then it burst into life like a small pulsing star.

'It's alive!' yelled Harriet. 'I didn't hurt it! It came alive!'

She wanted to shout at the top of her voice. She wanted to dance. She wanted to tell everyone. She had touched the Gift and in her own vulnerable human hand it broke into fiery blossom.

She lost all sense of time, following the winding paths. Everything was dark and formless except for the starry pulsing thing in her hand that guided her as surely as if it spoke, nudging her this way and that. She could not even see her own body, except her naked hand, itself curiously lit. But she sensed the familiar contours of herself and was not afraid.

I'm not lost in the maze. I'm found in it, she thought, a bubble of laughter and delight rising up inside her. *It's going to be all right. There's nothing to it, once you get the hang of it.*

Then the darkness drained away leaving in its place a cold dim undersea phosphorescence.

At the same moment the light in her hand went out.

'So this is as far as you go, is it?' she said to it, her heart contracting. 'I don't think much of that, frankly.'

As she looked about her, her consternation grew. This wasn't Gerard's Maze. No thunder, lightning, unearthly voices.

A little distance away a shadow loomed out at her, ancient: ominous as a standing stone. It's been here forever, thought Harriet, and for some reason this made her feel even worse.

Reluctantly she made her way towards it, realising as she approached that it was not a natural object after all but a giant archway carved not in stone, but in some unfamiliar kind of wood. The arch was stained and blackened as though someone had once tried to burn it down and there were heaps of ashes lying about. The air was unbreathable with the stink of old finished fires.

Beyond the arch rose a dizzy flight of stairs and at the top of the stairway she could just glimpse, with difficulty, a second door.

'It looks so cold and lifeless. This must be the most depressing place I've ever been to in my whole life.'

She compared the dreary scene with her fearful imaginings, and the reality was so much worse, so terrible in its desolation that she felt she would choke

224

on self-disgust. What had she thought she was up to? Nerving herself for who-knew-what heroics. Well, this was the end of it.

She sank down on to the scorched earth. What was the use of telling her to *choose* when all choices in the end were meaningless?

'The Door of Fire!' She laughed bitterly. 'And I fell for it. What a bad joke. And what do I tell Gerard? "I'm sorry, my trusty companion of the Quest, but I got there too late. The fire was out, you see."'

She heard a faint sound and turned sharply. Someone was watching her. A leaf-dappled child fled back into the gloom. Gerard's lost children. Wild half-children left behind while their blighted doubles went out to pretend to grow up, pass exams, rule the world.

Laurie, she thought, her heart breaking. Flora and my father. Lindsey. Me.

She held the Gift in her hands, tossing it to and fro between her gloved and ungloved hands. Why had it brought her here? Why had all her hopes been raised – for this? Had the tribal elders booted her out into the night and bullied her up her lonely mountainside only to mock and belittle her?

'Okay, wise old tribal woman,' she said desperately. 'If you're really in my head – tell me what to do? Go on – I dare you.'

She sat still, cross-legged amongst the reeking ashes, frowning with concentration, listening intently within herself. After a while, like a leaf blowing in through a window, a memory floated into her head.

Once when Harriet was about three or four, Caroline found her up in one of the Owlcote attics in a violent storm; perched on the window seat, her head stuck out of the open window, her hair plastered down with the downpour, glorying in the lightning, singing at the top of her voice.

Later she had learned to be afraid of being struck down by it like everyone else.

Everyone has a kind of earth energy that works best for them. Yours is fire. Will you accept it? Will you unbind it? The old woman's hands were quiet upon the skin drum, her eyelids closed.

'That's all right for you, old lady,' complained Harriet. Harriet knew enough about fire to understand that it changed what it touched and once it started there was no controlling it. Oh if you didn't ask for much, like Caroline. If you were happy in your suffocating kitchen, if you only needed it to boil eggs then it wasn't a problem, she thought hatefully.

But sometimes fires even start in kitchens.

And against her will she remembered in unrelenting detail the look on Caroline's face as she washed her bloody hands and the driven desperation on Avery's as he bolted from the little son who needed him. Perhaps Caroline had once believed kitchens were safe places.

But there is no safe place, she thought, and at this the old woman leapt to her feet in a shower of dust and began a slow stomping barefoot dance of triumph. *There's just the world as it is. Just places where you either choose to live or refuse to live . . .*

What would happen if I —

She put the Gift back into her pocket.

Probably nothing at all.

What harm could it actually do?

Remember how the lightning danced down the sky in all its colours.

She got to her feet. Breathing hard, biting her lip, she set her naked palm to the blackened wood. She was remembering how the pear tree pulsed under her hand as if it knew her. Commonplace phrases raced through her head, transformed to words of incantation, words of power.

Touching wood. Human touch. Golden touch. Which of these?

Somewhere the old woman was stamping her slow circling dance, her bracelets jangling, raising power, chanting along with her. On her ancient brown forehead she wore the design of a painted flame, contained within a daubed circle.

Which of these? Which of these? she asked Harriet impatiently.

'All of them,' Harriet answered. 'I can have all of them. They are all one.'

Find your fire self and unbind her!

There was a roaring sound under her feet. In terror she leapt back. Something brilliant burst out of the earth.

What have I done!

Lion-coloured flames leapt up the side of the archway. Within seconds the massive structure was ablaze.

What have I done? That door has been here forever. Now it's going to burn down and it will all be my fault. There won't be anything left of it. Why did I do it?

She was transfixed in terror. What kind of wood must it be to burn so swiftly, to smell so strange and sweet.

'I'm sorry,' she cried out, closing her eyes like a small child to shut out the awful reality of what she'd done, feeling the tremendous heat strike against her face like heat from an open oven. 'I'm sorry. Please make it stop!'

But still the infuriating old woman whirled in the dust, chanting, stomping, apparently tireless as if she was a force of nature and not human at all.

The fire was running along the earth away from her now in molten tracks between the arch and the stairway. With great cracklings and gusty detonations, with great golden bursts of exuberance the flames went dancing on up the stairs, up and up, until they had almost reached the second door.

What can I do?

Suddenly, even in the midst of her terror she understood something. The strangely carved wood of the giant archway was still unharmed. It was burning fiercely but – it was crazy but she had to admit that the arch actually seemed to acquiesce in its own burning. As if, like her maddening toothless wise old woman, it exulted in it, she thought, wondering.

And in the swimming golden haze Harriet saw that the carved wood had come alive! All its stiff wooden beasts and birds, its formal dancing men and women had sprung into extraordinary life. They were changing even as she looked at them, changing back and forth: men into centaurs, trees into women, children into birds, playfully taking on this form or that as if the fire moved them from within in some glorious spontaneous delight in *change itself*.

It was not destroyed in the inferno. It was healed. It was renewed. Again and again and again.

The old woman was suddenly still as a hunting cat; intently watching, waiting, haloed in a mazy circle of flame.

Touch wood. Human touch. Golden touch. All one.

'I don't – ' Hardly daring to believe, she edged closer to the arch, timidly holding out her bare hand to its blaze to feel the heat for herself.

Put your hand into the fire.

She no longer knew if the voice was in her head or in the maze.

Put your hand into the fire.

An expression of determination came into her face.

'I will,' she whispered. 'I will.'

She took off her spectacles and put them in her pocket. She braced herself. The dancing colours played upon her face. The heat stirred her hair.

Then, with love and terror, she thrust her naked hand deep into the heart of the flames until she could feel for herself the carved wood of the arch under her fingers. Cool, unconsumed and vibrant it was as living to her touch as the living trunk of the pear tree.

It doesn't burn me! It doesn't burn me! It is my own fire and cannot burn me. Oh glory be, glory be – it is my own fire!

She passed under the burning arch. The flames danced alongside her and ahead, tawny as marigolds. The same wind fanned them that blew her imprisoned hair, loosening it so that it blew back in a burnished cloud. She was at the foot of the stairway, a golden fire at her back and ahead, far ahead at the dizzy summit of the stairs, a dim blue incandescence. Harriet took a deep breath and began to climb.

Old Hatty woke with a start. Her heart was pounding like a jack hammer.

Something's happening in the maze.

'No,' she said. 'No, they've no right – Bertie forbids it.'

She swung herself painfully upright in her curtained bed and fumbled for her clothes.

'I'll put a stop to it,' she said.

20

Harriet Unbound

As she grew nearer the blue fire changed, becoming clearer, fiercer, burning like salt. She had never seen a blue so pure. Its blazing clarity played tricks on her eyes so that within the vibrance she began to see dazzling showers of other iridescent hues.

'Like a peacock's tail,' she whispered. 'I could never have imagined anything so lovely. But how do I get through?'

The first door had been an open archway.

But the second door was a wavering sheet of solid azure flame.

She approached it with increasing apprehension, trying to peer through to whatever lay invisibly beyond but it was like gazing into the depths of the fiery furnace in the Bible: fire within fire, spiral within fiery spiral. Impossible.

To thrust one hand into the fire was one thing, she thought. But to entrust her whole body, her whole self. That would be suicide.

In her panic she took a half step backwards. Then she shrieked out recoiling as a hissing cobra-head of flame leapt across the fiery stair, striking at her.

Tears of pain sprang to her eyes as she sucked her bare hand. A crescent of scarlet broke out on her flesh. She was trapped. She dared not go on. *But if I go back*

231

I'll be burned. She stood trembling, her eyes enormous in her terror.

All your gifts will turn to curses.

'But this isn't a choice!' she cried in a rage. 'I'll be incinerated whatever I do. This is a trick. A disgusting trick.' She sucked again at the searing pain in her hand. She was alone and she'd always been alone ever since she was left in the –

Wait a moment, she thought. Wait a moment. That's how I used to think. But I don't think like that any more. I've changed. This is just a boring old tape recording of who I used to be.

'Okay, old tribal lady,' she said, aloud. 'I know you only live inside my head, but I need you one more time. I'm stuck again. I don't know what to do.'

This time the old woman was in a grove of summer trees, by some kind of rushing yellow river, waiting for her. There were three other ancient crones with her, withered as late apples, with hardly a sound tooth between them, yet they could teach her grandmother a thing or two about old age, she thought.

Hurry up, said her own old woman, irritably. *Are you still hanging about on the stairs. You should have been here by now. Do I always have to spell everything out to you youngsters. Trust the fire and go forward. It's your own fire. If you keep going forward there's nothing to fear and everything to gain. Haven't you ever heard of a baptism of fire? Well, that's only your own fire self, unbound.* She turned away as if losing interest and began talking to her friends. They had set up a loom among the trees and were working on the last bright length of a complicated piece of cloth which absorbed all their attention.

Harriet took a faltering step towards the door of flowering fire but then shrank back piteously.

Walk through the fire of your terror.

She breathed deeply, gathering all her inner forces. Shaking in every limb, Harriet Noone walked forward into the fire.

Old Hatty buttoned herself into her black dress with stiff fingers that wouldn't obey her properly. Some of the buttons looked wrong when she had finished but she was decent, that was the main thing. *Something's happening in the maze.*

'But Bertie forbids it!' she cried.

People had no respect. Not for the dead and not for the living either. Well she would make them show respect. That devious mousy boy. That witch-faced girl. She knew exactly who was at the bottom of it. And she couldn't trust anyone but herself to take action. She felt dizzy and disorientated but it was no time to give in to physical weakness. Hatty Noone pushed back her shoulders and, for the first time in years, stormed out of the house.

Clothed in azure flame Harriet passed into the fire's heart. She retained a vague memory that she had been afraid of something, but could not recall what, for the strange thing was that when Harriet entered the fire, the fire also mysteriously entered Harriet. There was no division. No pain. She was no longer a terrified human girl. Entering the blazing dimensions of her own fire self, she shone with a steady blue-white radiance like a star.

She had entered the fire alone yet now she seemed surrounded by friendly, if indistinct, presences.

Ahead the burning blue became soft, lambent. She experienced a quickening, a kind of joy and she began to run. She thought she could run and run through this landscape forever and never be tired. She wanted it to go on forever; the benign presences wavering flame-like around her, the energy singing in her veins, the hyacinth-blue fire raining down, becoming ever softer, more delicate and translucent. Then without understanding how she had arrived there without first seeing it, she found herself standing before a third door.

It was white with a molten heat, whiter than burning lilies. It hurt her eyes to behold it. No other colours danced within its blinding radiance. There was something absolute and terrible about it. But without faltering she went steadily forward into the dazzling snowfire of the third and final doorway.

On the far side the ground fell away. At her feet was a chasm through which roared an immense rushing golden flood, too broad to leap over; its rapids of seething fire too perilous to wade through.

And on the opposite bank, four withered old women waited by moonlight under a spreading tree. Harriet's crone had a young owl perched peacefully on her shoulder and Harriet knew that the owl too had passed through transforming fires, shedding its nightmare plumage, its suffocating aspects, and now waited only for her, wild, shining, as friend and ally. The four crones stood as calmly rooted upon the earth as if they had been here forever, spinning and weaving the robe they had made. And now there was no doubt in her mind, only one single burning intent to cross the river and take what they held out to her. It was the most important thing in the world. All her life had been leading to this moment.

An old playground rhyme came back to her.

'Ferryman, ferryman will you take me across your Shining Golden River?' she whispered. Answering herself. 'Only if you give me your last glove.'

Peeling it off she hurled it from her and watched it fall into the boiling tide, consumed in the river of living gold.

Then: 'Ready or not – Here goes nothing!' she cried and taking a flying run she leaped triumphantly out into space.

Gerard had fallen into a fitful doze, at the kitchen table, his head among the dirty tea cups. In his dream he was lifted up into a dizzy place where he could see the entire Night Maze spread out like a living tapestry and Harriet was there, laughing at him, wearing some unfamiliar garment that dazzled his eyes so that he couldn't look at it properly.

'Look,' she called to him. 'Look at this!'

And she held out her arm and a young owl swooped down and balanced there, as bright as a phoenix, swaying, blinking solemnly at him with its wild wise eyes.

'Gerard, wake up. It's all right to come now.'

For a moment or two he stared vacantly around the kitchen trying to understand why he was here and what was happening. Her voice seemed to be calling him. The kitchen door had blown open while he slept.

Still groggy, his legs like an old man's, Gerard staggered out into the night, towards the maze, answering her huskily. 'Hang on, Harriet, I'm coming.'

The cold air revived him. And as the feeling came back into his cramped limbs he began to run without knowing why, without knowing how he would find his way amongst the paths now Harriet had the Gift.

'Harriet!' he called, as he ran. 'Harriet!'

Still calling her, he dived into the pitch-black alley between the looming walls of box and then the world began to shake to pieces around him.

21

Address:
the Universe

With a blast of incredible force, as though snatched up by a hurricane, the Night Maze spiralled off into space like a gigantic space ship, taking Gerard helplessly with it. Like a fly on a wall, he clung to the spinning maze, digging his fingers frantically into the earth, knowing that his last moments had come, trying not to look as roofs and treetops then clouds, later stars, planets hurtled by.

'Harriet!' he was still shouting. 'Harriet!' But the useless squeak of his voice was torn from his throat as they roared through the galaxy like a thunderstorm. He remembered the scrap of child's handwriting stuck in Lindsey's diary and thought wildly: *Gerard Noone, Owlcote Maze, Somewhere in the Universe.*

Then he was dumped down; dead, presumably, if he could only pull himself together sufficiently to take it in.

Then he thought: this is my dream! This was what it was like in my dream!

Recognising the astonishing thing that had just happened, he felt like a panicked cross between Dorothy in *The Wizard of Oz* and a god on Mount Olympus.

Below him, Thomas Noone's maze spread itself

amongst the stars, like a gigantic board game, a living labyrinth of darkness and light. But by some mysterious process, its every spiral twist and turn, no matter how far away, became instantly visible to his changed perception as soon as he focused upon it. He shook his head, awed. Then it struck him that he should be able to find Harriet easily enough when he needed to, just by wanting to. There were people moving about, he could see, in various costumes, times and weathers, coming and going in a kind of lovely ebbing flowing dance as though drawn by invisible tides.

'Gerard,' said someone softly behind him. He spun round. She was smiling at him, sitting on the ground, with a breathtaking backcloth of stars, scattered generously as daisies, the full skirt of her gingham dress pulled down over her feet; a girl with mouse-brown hair, dragged severely to one side with a plastic slide.

'I'm sorry I had to go,' she said, without fuss.

He knew who she was of course. It was sensible of her to remember to appear to him like that. Not wafting about in a long ghostly nightie. She looked more approachable this way; a friend and ally.

'Hallo,' he said. 'I did miss you a lot. But it's okay.'

There wasn't anything more that needed to be said since she knew everything that had happened as well as he did. They sat together in deep contentment for what may have been a long while. He couldn't tell; because it was timeless, he supposed. They may have been talking to each other without words because it wasn't an empty silence. But after a while, as though by common consent, they both moved, caught tearfully at each other's hands and then, laughing, pulled away at exactly the same moment, looking at each other with an understanding for which no words were needed.

'Look,' she said quietly.

He followed her pointing finger.

Into the centre of the maze ran Alice, skinny in her dirty linen undershift, a dark bottle clutched in her hand. She ran low, pressing herself against the hedge, as wild and strange as a child raised by wolves.

'We should do something!' cried Gerard, racked with guilt amidst his happiness. 'We can help her. She talked to me like she talked to you. It's our last chance. She keeps trusting us all and everyone fails her.'

'No,' said Lindsey. 'I can't explain it to you easily but it's like ripples from a dropped stone – can't you feel it?' She held out her arms and there was a strange rhapsodic expression on her face that reminded him of the wordless singing of the Doors of the Elements.

He fell silent again listening within himself and found that he could actually sense some new disturbance of the universe. Strong pulses of light and darkness beat upon him in rhythmic waves; each time the ripples spreading strongly further out, further back, not losing momentum, but gathering tremendous force.

'Harriet chose *herself*,' said Lindsey. 'She chose in trust and terror and out of the depths of her real nature. That was the dropping of the stone. The power she released is literally limitless. The ripples will go on forever, affect everything. If you set yourself free, Gerard, you free everything. Past, future, everything. And *everyone*.'

She looked at him, willing him to understand.

For a moment Gerard saw her as she had truly

239

become; so much more, infinitely more than a gawky schoolgirl in a gingham dress.

Lindsey Frances Noone. The Universe.

She was at home in the universe, at last. She really was. And he was her son.

'Now look again, Gerry,' she said, pointing to a different part of the maze. 'First things first.'

And there, storming between alleys of towering box came old Hatty Noone, all in black, more witch-like than ever.

'Now we need your Harriet,' said Lindsey and somewhat beyond being surprised, Gerard was merely interested to find that Harriet was now beside them, no longer in the dazzling robe of his dream, nor wearing her tame owl, but in her ordinary jumper and jeans. Her hair had broken out, that was the only change. Not the only change, but the only one he could put a name to.

'Have you got it?' Lindsey asked, holding out her hand. And almost formally Harriet put into it the moon-coloured ivory bobbin. Then Gerard noticed something else. Harriet's hands were bare, ungloved.

'I think it actually belongs to the old women,' Harriet said. 'Or whatever they really are. I think they were Doors when Gerard met them. They might be something else now. Trees or rocks or wild geese.'

'Don't worry, it's gradually working its way back to them, whatever shapes they choose to assume,' said Gerard's mother, and she laughed and looked affectionately at Harriet.

Then she turned again to Gerard and touched him on the shoulder, looking at him as if she knew him through

240

and through. He understood it was a leavetaking but felt no sadness. She would never really leave him now.

Then she gave the Gift a deft upward spin as if she was tossing a coin but at the last moment deliberately let it drop instead of catching it.

For a moment it teetered on its edge and Gerard thought it would go hurtling down amongst the stars like a ballbearing in a pinball game, but then, as though following a command, it went rolling smoothly along the narrow paths until it stopped dead at the feet of old Hatty Noone.

The old woman stopped in her tracks, scowling, her hand pressed to her side. She didn't seem to know where she was or why; like a spider knocked out of its web, a scuttling glowering old lady in rusty black. Then suddenly her eyes fastened in appalled recognition upon the bobbin and beyond it, to her daughter Lindsey, who stooped in front of her and picking it up, held it out to her mother unsmiling.

'You,' said Hatty harshly, afraid. 'How can *you* be here?'

'I stole this from you,' said Lindsey. 'I took what I needed. Now I'm giving it back. I didn't mean Avery to get the blame. He suffered enough from you as it is. I always thought he was the golden one, the luck child, being your favourite. But I was luckier than he ever was.'

Hatty didn't move. First anger then dread and bewilderment crossed her face. 'Why am I here? I don't remember – something was happening and I had to stop it but – Why am I here?' She pressed her hand to her side, gasping a little for breath.

'To choose,' said Lindsey. 'You just wouldn't choose,

241

Hatty. You should have chosen fire like Harriet but *they'd* made you so terrified you thought you had to hide yourself behind walls of earth with Bertie Noone, even though you never loved him even for a moment. You just wanted to lose yourself somewhere and Owlcote was the place you always ran away to when you were a child. Up in the pear tree you felt free to dream your dreams of escape to rain forests and cities of gold. And poor old Bertie was fool enough to offer marriage. And you thought it served him right if he couldn't tell the difference between love and safety. You twined your little feminine fingers into his lapels like poisoned ivy and smiled sweetly and tearfully into his face, and the two of you walked out of the maze arm in arm among the summer roses and the gramophone was playing "Tea for Two" and that was that. That was the two of you done for.

'And then you were married and you had Avery and you thought that, if Bertram Noone couldn't be the saving of you, your firstborn son would have to be. He would love you the way no one else ever had. He would be your crock of gold under the rainbow. You could send him out into the world to be what you'd always been too scared to be. Only it didn't work – if he was ever to please you he had to lose himself. He had to turn himself into your puppet and a puppet wasn't what you wanted. You wanted a hero. And then came poor Will, stuck in the middle, scared to say Boo in case you ate him alive. And then there was me, the sly one, the tricky one, the cuckoo child. All I ever wanted was for you to love me, you know, Hatty. But you couldn't even stand to look at me, could you? Because whenever you did you saw – '

242

'Don't – oh don't. How could you know that, when I couldn't ever bring myself to tell another human soul. It was myself I saw in your face. I knew you were only biding your time, hiding your hatred behind your sly ways. You were me all over again,' said Hatty, trembling. 'That was my curse. My stubborn self reborn in you. Everything I'd ever tried to hide and smother in myself. The self that used to kick and scream with defiance at what they tried to turn me into. They'd shut me on the cellar stairs alone, screaming for hours in the dripping darkness. Father would say, "She must learn self-control, Mother." And Mother would take to her bed with a headache: "I'm too delicate for all this unpleasantness." At least when they hurt me I knew I was still real enough to fight back. But when he laughed at me – that shrank me down smaller than a candle flame. Then when he'd shrunk and bullied me down into nothing, when they'd made me small enough to fit into the suffocating space they called being "a good daughter", they told me I was grown up and would have to go out into the world. What could I do then? What was the use of trying. They'd finished me off.'

'Nothing's finished. Nothing's lost,' said Lindsey quietly. Her words rang out through the air, and reaching Harriet and Gerard went on resonating through and beyond them with a warm brazen sound as though a gong had been struck.

'We can't lose ourselves even if we try. Only mislay them, for a time. I keep trying to tell you. You can choose again. Everything is still here. The false gold and the living gold. The riddle and its answer. The curse and its healing. Everything that lives. Earth, Water, Fire, Air.'

'How the blue blazes can I choose again?' howled Hatty. 'It's all over. Has been for years. Trapped in time like flies in amber. The past a doom. The future a coming terror. The present a frail raft of matchsticks in between. One wrong decision when you're weak and young and silly and before you know it, whole families falling through space like dominoes. I wish I'd had more courage. But I didn't and that's the truth of it. Don't torture me. How can I choose again?'

But Lindsey was walking away from her calmly, the stars burning around her head and beneath her feet. 'I wanted to help you,' she said over her shoulder. 'For some reason children always want to heal their parents. I always loved you though, Hatty. You may as well know it now.'

'Wait!' cried Hatty. 'Wait for me – wait. Please wait. Don't leave me here by myself.'

With difficulty she began to run, between walls that even now were changing, shifting; over ground that was rippling like wheat, became flowing like water.

'Wait!' she called in agony. 'Please don't go – I need you,' she cried, holding out her arms.

Slowly, slowly, Lindsey turned.

For an age while Harriet and Gerard watched, afraid to breathe, she turned and turned in a swirl of gingham, and for an age old Hatty ploughed towards her, her lungs exploding with effort.

'Take me with you,' the old woman wept. 'Let me try – let me – please, let me love you.'

Something is happening!

At the heart of the maze, Alice halted, the open phial in her hand. She was dizzy and frightened. For one

244

moment everything had shivered as if the world was unmaking and remaking itself before her eyes. She could hear a voice calling her name.

She stared in bewilderment at the dark bottle, her trance broken. Moments before she had known what she was going to do with it. Fumes, as of something rotting, rose from its open mouth. It had seemed to offer a way out that was as easy as lying down in the snow and falling asleep. She had thought: *he loves gold. I will swallow his elixir and then I will become gold. At least he will love me in death.*

But now she looked at it in dread. In all her confused nights of dreams and visions it had never been like this. Could dreams change?

'Alice – oh God, please, I love you! Alice, damn you – answer me!'

Then to her disbelief the disembodied voice broke into song in a great hurting, cracking off-key tremor.

'Earth, Fire, Water, Air. Met together in a garden fair. Put in a basket bound with skin – '

'If you answer this riddle,' she muttered, her lips cracked and dry. 'You'll never . . . Father?' she whispered.

For so long nothing had been quite what it seemed. Ghosts had more substance than brothers and sisters. Wild beasts came to her when her human father could not bear her presence. The seasons blurred. Falling whiteness might be snow or blossom. Voices sounded in her head when no one was near. Could this really be her father?

She looked down at herself, her stained linen, the verminous bites on her calves, her unhealed sores. Had she not grown too wild and strange to be any man's daughter? Could she still love him or was her father, once so beloved, only a cruel stranger now? But her heart leapt within her as if it would speak for her. He had cried 'I love you' into the darkness. He had known her song. She heard him blunder up against a blind alley, cursing.

'Father, Father – ' she cried in terror and love to guide him. 'I am here.'

The maze was golden, incandescent.

Hatty and Lindsey were the centre of a burning golden whirlpool.

They stretched out their hands. Their fingers touched.

Thomas Noone staggered into the centre of the maze. Slowly, slowly, her eyes always warily fixed on his smoke-smeared face, Alice went towards him, and the alchemist, with an expression of mingled dread and desire, took another stumbling step towards his daughter. Then, like two magnetised objects that stray too close, no longer able to choose whether to stay or go, they stumbled together in an awkward rush of human flesh and bone.

Thunder cracked. The maze tilted, spun. The stars wheeled like birds overhead and underfoot. In another world a child cried out. Shocked and awed, Krake looked down at the body of old Mrs Noone, lying where she had collapsed on to her bed in her half-buttoned dress. With mute respect she covered her face.

Laurie's eyes fluttered, his eyes opened and he pushed away the oxygen mask. 'Don't be silly,' he said in his growly gravelly four-year-old voice. 'I can breathe all by myself now. The owl's gone away. Harriet made friends with it and she told it to. Can we go home?'

Gerard and Harriet stood in a grey rainswept garden watching them go: Alice and Thomas Noone, father and daughter, hand in hand into the house.

As they were lost to view Gerard thought he heard behind him, the sound of children's voices, a ripple of excitement, a burst of smothered laughter in the leaves. He turned but there was no one. Whoever it was had gone.

'They've been set free too,' said Harriet. 'Don't worry. They've gone where they belong.'

Then the garden shivered like a reflection in a wind-stirred pool and they knew themselves to be wholly in their own time and place.

It was almost sunrise. Slowly, like drowned islands, trees and shrubs were rising out of the flowing formless mist.

'I never realised before,' said Harriet, 'how stupid it was to have only one word for grey. It's an entire spectrum, look! I can see at least a thousand different kinds. Isn't it brill!'

She began to laugh, running across the soaking grass through a drizzling English dawn. In the west the sky theatened a further downpour. The air was charged with electricity.

'There's going to be one almighty storm,' said Gerard. 'You know,' he said shyly to her, 'you're just the same Harriet, but you're different too. Can you talk about it or is it too private?'

'I think it might be private for the time being,' said

Harriet. 'But if ever I do tell anyone, I should think it'll be you.'

'I had a dream while you were in the Night Maze,' he said. 'You were wearing a robe. I couldn't look at it, it hurt my eyes so much. And you called me to come and find you.'

'The old women made it for me,' Harriet said, relenting. 'And I put it on. All the elements were in it. And then it sort of dissolved, became part of me, I suppose. I suppose I must be wearing it now.' She shrugged her amazement at him, pulling a face and then immediately afterwards beaming at him. 'I'm afraid to say too much,' she admitted, 'in case all the glory leaks out of it and I find out that crushing juniper berries makes one prone to hallucinations.'

'You called the owl to you and it came,' he said enviously.

'Yes,' she said, her eyes shining. 'Yes! And Laurie's all right. I know he is.'

And then, looking past him, she gave a sudden piercing shriek that curdled his blood. 'Gerard – Bee's here!'

As she spoke Gerard registered the clattering smoke-filled arrival of a black Volkswagen with a trailing exhaust. At the same moment Will's door flew open and Will, his hair on end, came tearing down the stable steps like a maniac. Bee was climbing out of her car, wearily stretching herself, yawning, then flinched slightly as lightning forked lavender-blue above the park.

His cousin was already off like the wind, her hair a streaming banner, racing towards them. There was a faint thunderclap followed by a stumbling sound like a drum-kit falling down a distant flight of stairs, and the gentle drizzle suddenly turned to a solid sheet of freezing water. Gerard battled along behind her, trying to keep up, vainly calling out, 'Harriet, they might want to be – don't you think we should – '

But Harriet who had passed through fire, to whom an ordinary wet grey dawn had become a choral symphony, was not to be cheated of paradise now.

'Bee,' she carolled joyfully, ignoring him, as the lightning whizzed overhead, and the driving rain poured into her eyes and mouth, 'Bee, you came back! Oh, Bee – please, please do marry him this time!'

22

The Future Rose

'Well,' said Norah hoarsely, gesturing with her empty champagne glass at the musicians gravely playing Mozart in dappled midsummer sunlight on the lawn, 'do you think you could struggle to come to terms with all this eventually, you poor boy, if you really made an effort?'

Errol swung from Norah's free arm, completely tongue-tied. He had hardly spoken to Gerard since he had arrived at Owlcote, thunderstruck to see his old friend in such grand surroundings.

'We don't usually have the musicians,' said Gerard, in case she was getting a somewhat false impression of his new life. 'They're friends of Lottie's. They just came for the free food. They had to borrow the suits.'

'Well, that is a relief,' said Norah drily. Then she burst out laughing at Gerard's slightly wounded expression. 'Oh, Gerry – I'm so happy for you. You just don't know how I worried about you after you left. In case you secretly hated me for letting you in for a new family.'

Just as he was about to answer her, Harriet came racing up, the trailing long skirt of her bridesmaid's dress carelessly hitched up in one hand. She had discarded her Juliet cap as soon as she decently could but her hair fell in a blue-black waterfall down her back and amongst the curls seed pearls glistened like caught raindrops. Galloping up behind her came Laurie and Flora in rather grass-stained wedding finery, their faces glowing like peonies. The soft pensive music suddenly changed into a lively air, like an old-fashioned country dance.

'These are my cousins,' said Gerard shyly, as he saw the two broken halves of his world come smoothly together around him to form a strange and wonderful circle. 'This is – '

'I knew you had to be Norah,' interrupted Harriet. 'Wasn't it lovely of you to come so far just to see boring old Gerard. Still the food isn't bad and the music's quite nice – Aha!' She pounced behind Norah where Errol was skulking, panicked by this overpoweringly exuberant vision in peach silk. 'You can't hide from me. You're Errol, aren't you? You're the boy who gives fantastic birthday presents – aren't I right? Wasn't it you?'

At this Errol risked a wintery smile and a small frightened nod.

'Well, come on then,' she said holding out her hand. 'Everyone's going to dance and Flora hasn't got a partner.'

Errol inched out from Norah's shadow but before he could change his mind Flora marched up to him, round-eyed and stiff with seriousness under a lopsided wreath of rosebuds, clamping his hand firmly within her own. Then off they careened in a wild skipping dance in which Flora did not once forget to point her toes as she had been taught in her ballet class.

'And I suppose I must be stuck with you,' said Harriet fondly to her brother. 'Yuck, Laurie, what have you been eating? Your hands are disgustingly sticky.'

251

And Gerard heard Laurie say gloatingly as they swung off across the sunlit grass: 'Everything. Everything. Something of abserlootly everything.'

'May I have the honour?' said Will strolling up, looking surprisingly handsome in his morning suit.

'Well,' said Norah, a little pink with the champagne. 'It's not every day you get asked to dance in an Elizabethan garden. I'd hate to miss a unique experience.'

'You're looking thoughtful, Gerry,' said Bee appearing at his side in a dazzling ivory creation and eating a strawberry with her fingers. 'What a dreadful crush, isn't it? I wanted a quiet do. This is all Caroline's fault. Don't you just hate all the little stunned things on toast and the little damp *suspect* things camouflaged in flaky pastry? I bet Caroline and Lottie would have produced something much nicer left to themselves.'

'Uncle Avery said they had to get proper caterers,' said Gerard. 'He said she'd have too much else to do. She was so excited you agreed to have the wedding here. She's really potty about having you properly in the family.'

'And what a much improved family it is nowadays,' said Bee, enjoyably licking her fingers clean. 'Even Avery is disturbingly human, I've noticed. Let's go and find them, shall we, Gerry, and drag them off into the merry dance.'

Avery and Caroline had escaped down to the river and were walking along the bank, heads close together.

'I suppose I must have been asleep,' Avery was saying. 'I suppose it was a dream but I've never had a dream like it. In fact I don't think I've remembered a dream in years. It was more of a nightmare to start with. This little kid struggling horribly nearby in the dark where it had fallen in the water. Flooded mine workings, something like that, it must have been. I hate the water, Carrie. I've always been terrified of drowning. I kept hoping someone else would turn up and pull him out. But there was only me and he kept going under for longer and longer. It was desperate. So in the end – I just sort of dived in and managed to grab hold of him before he went down for the last time and dragged him out. And he was – well, I think it was a close thing. I could see he mightn't pull through on his own. I had to breathe into his mouth and really work on him to get him breathing properly for himself. And then I got really panic-stricken in case, after all that he wasn't going to survive.' He gave a shaky laugh.

'But he did,' said Caroline. 'He did or you wouldn't be telling me.'

'How do you know what I'm going to say,' he said incredulous. 'You know, don't you?'

She shrugged and smiled and bit her lip, abruptly looking away over the flowering blue and gold irises, her eyes filling. 'Tell me anyway.'

'I don't think I can describe what it felt like. It's just that he suddenly opened his eyes and looked at me with such – well, relief and recognition. Well, I suppose you would say, love. And I thought, good heavens it was Laurie. It was poor little Laurie in the water all the time. But then just as he threw his arms around me I realised he was – he was – '

'He was you,' said Caroline, still looking away over the water.

'I was so ashamed,' he said in a low voice. 'When Laurie – I was terrified. I didn't know what to do. You seemed so *sure* and I – I can't bear to remember – '

'I know,' she said. 'Don't. It's all right.' And she groped for his hand blindly.

'You sneaky low-down pair,' cried Beatrice a few minutes later. 'Why should you married old people have any privacy at my wedding! Right, Avery – just the man I wanted.' And she seized the astonished Avery's hand and relentlessly hauled him off to join the dance which seemed to be steadily gathering momentum.

'Oh,' said Caroline, her eyes still bright. 'Isn't everything lovely. Come on, Gerard. Shall we join the others?'

They sped off together hand in hand.

In and out of the flowering borders the dancing figures wove: Beatrice and Avery were just in front of them. Further ahead still, they saw Norah and Will vanish into a green alley between tall hedges of smoothly manicured box.

'I hope poor old Hatty won't mind now,' said Caroline as they went whirling after the others into the sunlit green.

'She doesn't,' said Gerard. 'I know she doesn't.'

But he only smiled secretively when she asked him how he could be so sure.

Ahead of them couples whisked off to right and left.

'If we take this path we'll get straight to the heart of the maze before any of them,' he said competitively, tugging his aunt down a different route altogether.

And moments later they arrived alone in the centre of the maze where they reeled at last to a standstill, giggling and out of breath.

Then Gerard's jaw dropped.

'The rose,' he said. 'Wherever did – ?'

Caroline laughed. 'You look as if you've seen a ghost. It's only a rose. Nothing in the slightest bit supernatural. With my own scarred muddy little gardener's hands I dug the hole and put in the muck and bonemeal and potash. Then I brought the rose back from the nursery and I planted it. Don't you like it? It was obliging of it, I thought, to burst so enthusiastically into flower for the wedding, wasn't it?'

But the summer maze, the approaching clamour of the dancers, his aunt's voice, all faded into a meaningless jumble around him as he gazed and gazed at the vision of Caroline's ordinary shrubby rose bush starred all over with delicate flowers of gold.

'It's not an old-fashioned one,' his aunt was saying. 'I decided I was far far too obsessed with trying to recreate the past. Doves in dove cotes and sixteenth-century gardens. Anyway, old roses get every blight that's going. So this is a truly modern blight-free rose. It smells lovely though, doesn't it? I was afraid it mightn't have a smell.'

'It's the future rose,' said Gerard when he could speak. 'I've smelled it before.'

For a moment he had his old queasy carsick feeling as all around them, the camouflage of time trembled. And as the wedding guests came noisily weaving around them, in and out of the leafy arches, the maze seemed to be thronging with people, visible and invisible: past, present and to come.

And he wished he could explain to Caroline how the perfume of this ordinary rose had woven itself so extraordinarily into the private stuff of his hopes and dreams, ever since as a small boy, alone in a room full of shadows, he had first allowed himself to imagine Lark.

Now he had arrived in that child's future and it had become his own present. And the present stretched away in each and every possible direction, as shining, as spacious, as magical as his eye could see and his heart imagine.